WARNING:

The following book has many scenes which some will find offensive and disturbing. If you are not a fan of extreme horror and are easily shocked and offended, please do not purchase this title.

This is an extreme horror novel intended for a mature audience only.

The characters and situations in this book are entirely fictional; the products of twisted minds.

A CIP catalogue record for this book is available from the British Library

ISBN-10: 1507773420

ISBN-13: 978-1507773420

MONSTER

For Christina Cooper,

May the nightmares within this book plague your dreams.

SHAW / BRAY

A Note From The Authors

Matt Shaw:

It's not often I start the book with one of these but, in this instance, I believe it is only fitting. One of 'these' being an apology. I am sorry for what you're about to read. Not because it is a bad story. I don't believe that. Had it been, I wouldn't have released it. The apology has more to do with the content.

When I first approached Michael Bray to write 'Monster' with me, I knew in my head what I wanted; or rather I knew the basics of what I wanted. He asked what I wanted from him and so I emailed him a rough structure of the story and the bits he needed to write. We alternated writing parts of the book, just as we did with ART. It was a system that worked well for us and we were keen to see if it would work again. When we had all the parts completed, we slotted it together like a big jigsaw!

My original idea was not to make this a Black Cover Book. I wanted it to have a proper cover and, although a bit horrible in places, appeal to a wider - more mainstream - horror audience. But then I started writing it. I got some dark ideas for the story pretty early on and emailed Bray about them. I didn't stop there, I mentioned them to other trusted sources too and the replies all came back the same; harrowing, 'fucking hell', 'holy shit', nasty and "What is wrong with you?" I didn't think much of these responses though. My idea was for the climax of the book, the big turning point, and people know I don't tend to beat around the bush with my endings. I like to make an impact, I like to make you sit up and question your morals and what you've just read. I want to get a reaction from you and this - this scene - gets a reaction. So, in my eyes, it's a winner. At this stage, I thought we could still release as a non-black cover title but chuck a warning on the front of it.

But then Michael started writing his sections and emailing me with ideas he had for his bits. I take full responsibility for the settings he writes but none for the content. I wanted him to do a back story for two of the characters and he took it somewhere extremely dark and bleak. Somewhere that even made me feel uncomfortable. I won't pretend I am not worried about certain scenes within this book. My horror is very much 'make- believe', the horror Bray touches upon in this title are the horrors faced in the real world. It's nasty and it's entirely possible people could have gone through them themselves. Do not start thinking Michael has written these scenes just for shock value though. He hasn't. They are key to the plot and help move the story forward and give understanding to the parts happening in the 'present day' situations (the first person sections I am writing). Without the horrors Michael has written - in detail - about, the story wouldn't be as good or interesting. It's as simple as that.

I have aired my concerns with people close to me who've asked why I don't edit the scenes Michael is writing. Quite simply - it is not my place to do so. I am not about to edit the words of a talented author. I am not about to delete things he has put to paper because I believe - together - we're pushing the boundaries so far past the line of decency that the line no longer exists in our world. I'd say something if it weren't key to the story but it is. It is a necessary evil and one he has written expertly.

Readers once told me there is no such thing as 'too far' when it comes to horror. Well - read this book and then pretend I've asked the question again. Are there parts of this that have gone too far and made you feel uncomfortable? The weird thing is - parts of me hopes that the answer is 'yes'. We are horror authors. We want to bring the horror to your world.

We just don't want to upset you.

It's a fine line we tread.

I am proud of the story itself. It is dark and bleak. Quite funny really when you consider the fact that - at the start of the writing process - I told Michael, and a few other people, that it wouldn't be as dark as ART, the other book we wrote together. I guess Michael and I are bad influences on one another.

Is that a bad thing though?

Michael Bray:

I wasn't entirely sure what I was going to write for these notes. In fact, I wasn't even sure I was going to write anything at all, however I think it's important that I touch upon some of the subject matter I have covered when writing my sections of this story.

Those who know my work will be aware that I am primarily a psychological horror author, which makes the places I had to go to during my sections of the story so difficult to approach. There are passages in here where on more than one occasion I stopped writing and asked myself if I really wanted to commit those words to the page. Almost entirely (one scene aside which Matt and I decided went just *too* far), everything made it into the manuscript.

The things you are about to read will raise a few questions as to the reason for their inclusion. As difficult as they were to write, I think the content is justified. Sometimes the hardest things to touch on for a fiction author are the things a little too close to real life to cause real discomfort. The situations within this story are ones which I am more than aware are a reality for a lot of people in their daily lives and as a result may blur the lines between fiction and reality.

This isn't a case of me trying to glorify those particular issues, or to give any kind of justification for those who perpetrate them. I did (and do) worry that people may be offended to the point of hating the story, to which I say please don't. The warning on the front is there for a reason, and if you are reading this, you have already made the commitment to take the risk and see what we have for you.

I think it's important as an author to keep pushing boundaries and testing yourself, especially when it comes to going outside of the usual comfort zone. Matt is a prime example of this. He continues to push boundaries with every release. The fact that some of the things I contributed to this story even made him uncomfortable speaks volumes. I was given complete freedom to craft my sections in the way I saw fit and really flesh out some of the characters you are about to read. As difficult as some of it may be to digest, I genuinely feel that it isn't a gimmick or a means to cause controversy. It's there because it is needed to move the story forward. Hopefully as you read, you will appreciate why we went the way we did with the content, and by the end might even have a better overall experience for it.

I think Matt and I are in agreement that we would rather push these boundaries and risk making you, the reader, uncomfortable in the face of the content, than play it safe and give you a book without that same kind of emotional journey and ultimate payoff. After all, isn't that the purpose of any creative medium, be it film, music, or writing?

In closing, I hope that you get at least something out of this book and appreciate why we took the journey we did during its creation. Be it repulsion, sadness, discomfort or anger, any emotional reaction, I'm of the opinion that any of these things serves to show that we were correct in the decisions we made, and if I had to go back and do it all again, I wouldn't change a thing because I have absolute faith that we did the right thing.

As always, working with Matt has been as easy as when we worked on Art. We seem to have a very natural organic rhythm when it comes to working together, and can tune in to the vibe the other is aiming for with very little in depth planning or conversation. I hope this book gives you the opportunity to step into the darkest parts of our collective minds, and let us take you to places I very much doubt you have ever been before.

MONSTER

P R O L O G U E

Large, clumsy fingers fiddled with a small, silver crank attached to the box in the sweaty palm of the other hand. A large shape, partially consumed by the darkness of the room, rocked excitedly where it perched on a rickety chair over in the corner. Rocking backwards and forwards, a wheezy laugh escaped deformed lips hidden beneath a mask made of stinking flesh. With each turn of the crank, more of *Ring around the Roses* played into the room, drowning out the frequent drips of water splashing the concrete floor from ripped holes in the damp ceiling of the old building. Something clicked within the dirty box and the lid flew open - pushed by a rotten severed hand attached to a spring. The large shape jumped and howled with fear before throwing the box across the room where it smashed against the far wall. In another room, down a dark, dingy corridor - someone else was also screaming.

#

I called out again, "Hello?" I know someone else is here. I can hear them screaming somewhere within the same building. "Hello?" The scream suggests they could be here against their will, like me. Maybe they're cuffed to a pipe on the wall as well? It would make sense as to why they're not coming but it wouldn't stop them from calling back to me, letting me know that they heard me. Letting me know that I'm not alone. How did I end up here? Last thing I remember was leaving the bar. Did I pass out? No. I couldn't have done. I was a little worse for wear but no worse than usual and I've certainly drunk more. If anything, this evening…Is it even the same evening? How much time has passed since being unconscious and waking to find myself here? I screamed again, "Can you hear me?" Somewhere I heard a door slam. "Hello? Please! I need your help! Hello?" If the door slammed, it means they're not stuck like I am. It means they're moving around. They're out there, free, and I'm in here stuck. They can help me. They must be able to help me. "Hello?!" I screamed again, louder than before. I froze, hoping to hear someone call back to me. Hoping to hear someone shout back that they heard me and not to panic, they're on their way. No one called back. I'm alone. Fuck.

I looked around the room again in the hope of finding a way out. I'd already wasted so much time looking for an escape and knew there wasn't one, at least not one that involved a key to undo the damned cuff clamped around my bruised wrist. The room is practically empty: a concrete floor, metal pillars holding up an unsafe looking ceiling, a hole in one of the floorboards above me, rusted pipes dotted along the walls - some of them banging and clanking for why I'm not sure. There's a broken chair in the middle of the room; one of the legs snapped off and the chair is lying on its side. And that's it. Nothing to help me out of my predicament. I screamed again, not to get attention this time but out of frustration. Someone - within the other rooms of this God forsaken building - mimicked my scream as though mocking me.

R Y A N

1.

"Are you still there?" Jema asked. She was on the other end of the phone pressed to Ryan's ear. He nodded in answer to her question before realising he needed to speak too; a visual acknowledgement being worth nothing over the telephone.

"Yes."

"Are you okay?"

He fell silent again as he just sat there, staring at the wall opposite his cluttered work desk. The clock - hung in the centre of the wall - had stopped. Its second hand not moving; time had frozen. Ryan was looking at it wondering whether there was anyway to wind it back to before the call came through; back to before he'd answered it.

"Ryan?" Jema sounded nervous, not that Ryan had noticed. Other than the frozen clock hanging on the wall, he'd noticed very little since taking the call. "Please talk to me," Jema continued.

"I'm sorry," he said before continuing, "you've kind of taken me by surprise."

Ryan and Jema had been dating for three months. Despite how they'd initially met, they'd discussed taking things slowly. Jema had been single for a while now and Ryan had only recently come out of a long-term relationship; a relationship he'd ended as he felt as though it weren't going anywhere. They'd met via mutual friends at a house party and one thing had led to another. Before their first date, they'd drunkenly slept together and it was because of this moment that Jema was phoning him.

"You're sure?"

"Two tests. A doctor's appointment confirmed it. They think I'm close to three months."

"And…" Ryan stopped himself. Jema noticed.

"What is it?" she asked. Ryan didn't answer her. She could hear him breathing down the other end of the phone. There'd only be one thing he was uncomfortable to ask and she knew exactly what it was. "It's yours," she said, putting him out of his misery and saving him from having to ask the awkward question.

"That's…good," he said, unsure of how best to respond. He'd felt the last relationship wasn't going anywhere. He'd been with the girl for eight years and although they shared a flat together, their lives were pretty much separate other than the odd date night during the week. If he was to be in a relationship, especially now that he was in his early thirties, he felt as though it needed to be going somewhere. Of course he realised the lack of progress on the last relationship was also down to him but he didn't feel comfortable asking for the girl's hand in marriage and he wasn't about to ask just for the sake of it. He didn't want to become another statistic, like his own mother and father had been when they divorced during his turbulent teenage years. That being said - a potential baby only three months into a new relationship, where they hadn't even moved in with each other, seemed to be moving too damned fast.

"Are you free tonight?" Jema asked.

"Tonight?"

"Yes. I thought we could talk."

"Talk?"

"I think we have things to talk about, don't you?" she asked. It had only been three months since the start of their relationship but Jema felt, for her at least, it was more than a fleeting romance. She liked Ryan and she was sure he liked her too. The baby wasn't planned, and she didn't want him to feel trapped by it, but - from finding out about the pregnancy - she'd already decided that she wanted it. It didn't help that - before she made the discovery - her mother often teased her that her body clock was ticking and ticking and ticking and that, soon, the batteries would die - just as they had on the wall clock in Ryan's office. "Well?" she pushed him for an answer. It would be nice to do this as a couple but, if need be, she'd go it alone. Being raised by a single mum hadn't hurt her when she was growing up, after her dad walked out when Jema was only three years old. "Ryan?"

"Sure," he said. "I'm free tonight. What time did you want to come over?"

Jema breathed a short sigh of relief. There was a part of her that honestly worried he was just going to break it off with her over the phone. They were new in the relationship and she understood neither of them had signed on to become parents yet. She was fully aware that his acceptance to meet up for a chat was not a confirmation that he wanted to be a father though and there was much to be discussed.

"I can get there for about eight?"

"Eight is good."

"Did you want me to bring anything?" she asked, unsure of how best to end the conversation.

"Just yourself," he answered.

She hesitated a moment before asking, "Can you at least give me a clue as to how you're feeling about this?"

"Look, I'm sorry but I'm at work - I appreciate you calling to tell me the news but can we finish this tonight?" he asked.

"Okay," Jema felt herself well up. Ryan immediately regretted saying it so abruptly but the truth of the matter was - he didn't know how he felt. Him? A father? It hadn't been something he'd really given much thought to. In his head, babies came after marriage and - as he hadn't even proposed to someone - he figured he still had time to stress about whether he was ready or not at a later date.

"I'll chat later," he said.

"Okay."

"I love you," he said. He did love her. But, again, a baby?

"I love you too. I'm sorry."

"I'm as much to blame as you are," he said. "Talk later." He hung up the phone and realised what he said.

Stupid idiot, he thought, *I should have told her there was nothing to apologise for.*

Too late now. Damage done.

He put the phone down on his desk and put his head in his hands. And to think, it had been such a good day up to this point.

His colleague called over from the desk opposite, "Any danger of you doing some work today?" he asked. Ryan stood up, pulled his coat from the back of the chair and walked from the room, leaving his colleague flummoxed. "Ryan?" The office door slammed shut behind Ryan. His colleague, Jim, grabbed his own coat and followed.

"Where are you going?" asked one of the other office workers. None of them were managers, they were all employed to do the same thing: take the incoming calls from the customers and help them with their queries.

"If anyone comes, just tell them I'm on a cigarette break," said Jim as he too disappeared through the door after his friend. Jim ran down the corridor which led to the lifts and stairs. The office was on the first floor so neither he nor Ryan ever bothered getting the lift. He ran straight past it and down the stairs, catching up with Ryan easily. "Ryan, wait!" he called out. Ryan didn't stop; he got to the bottom of the stairs and walked through the fire doors towards the building's main entrance, where the smokers all gathered during the day. Jim caught up with him out by one of the smoking points. "What's wrong with you?" he asked. "I'm guessing that call wasn't business related?"

"She's pregnant!" Ryan blurted out as he pulled a cigarette packet from his jacket's inside pocket. "I'm going to be a dad!"

"Pregnant? Who?" Jim asked, reaching for his own smokes.

"Who do you fucking think?" Ryan lit his cigarette and took a deep drag on it.

"Jema?"

"Yes fucking Jema! She just called me, knowing I was at work, and told me she's fucking pregnant! A baby! Me? A dad?"

Jim hesitated, "Congratulations?" he said, unsure of what the best thing to say was. Usually, when someone announced they were expecting a child, it was apt to say something like that but - in this instance - he wasn't sure. It would have definitely been easier to decide had Ryan been jumping up and down with joy.

"Do I look like I'm ready to be a dad? I don't know the first thing about fatherhood. It's not as though I learned a lot from my own old man." Despite Ryan's mum and dad separating when he was fairly young, he still saw his father fairly regularly, certainly more so than some children in a similar situation. But when he did see him, his father appeared as more of a businessman, ready to offer advice, as opposed to a father who was there to give unconditional hugs and fun-filled day trips to the beach or arcades.

"Don't you two use protection?" Jim asked. "I mean, if you're not ready to be a father…"

"Yes. We use protection," Ryan snapped. He was irritated Jim had followed him out. All he wanted was a little quiet time, with a cigarette, to process what he'd been told on the phone. He didn't need questions from his friend, even if his friend was - in his own way - trying to be there for him.

"Well I hate to ask this then but are you sure…"

"It's mine." Ryan took another drag on his cigarette. "When we first met each other we were both drunk and one thing led to another and…"

"No protection?"

"No. No protection."

"Ah."

"Yes. Ah. A fucking baby!"

"Well it could be a good thing?"

"Can it? I mean can it really? We've only been dating for a few months. And how can she have just found out she is pregnant? She would have known the first month that she missed a period, wouldn't she?"

"I'd presume so, yes, but not being a woman - I'm not too familiar with how all of that works I'm sorry to say. Has she been to the doctors?"

"Apparently so. She said she is around three months pregnant so it's not even a case of missing one period. She must have known something was happening. I mean, if we choose to get rid of it - can we even do that at this stage or is this a definite thing now? Whether I want it or not, I'm going to be a father and the only thing we need to discuss is whether I'm going to be a dad who is there for the kid every day or whether I'm going to be a father on paper who sees his kid on the weekends? Fuck." He froze.

"What is it?"

Ryan turned to Jim, "Do you think she knew before today and kept it to herself? Do you think she's trapping me? Shit."

"Honestly, mate, I don't know. I mean - it's entirely possible she could have just found out herself today. You read reports on women who go through the whole pregnancy without knowing they're pregnant so... Honestly, I don't know. You're just going to have to talk to her."

"I don't know what to say to her. What would you say?"

"I don't know - probably the same sort of thing you're saying now. Three months, you say? Did you not think she was getting bigger or anything?"

"She doesn't look pregnant. I mean, she looks a tiny bit bigger but not much. I just thought she was happy. Girls get fat when they're happy, right? That's a thing, I'm sure of it. They settle down with the man they believe to be 'the one' and they let themselves go."

"Or get pregnant to ensure they get a ring on their finger."

"Fuck you."

"I'm just pulling your leg. Honestly, this could be a great thing. This could be the best thing that has ever happened to you. I mean - don't get me wrong - it could also be the worst but..."

"Seriously - shut up."

"So what's next?" Jim asked, finally sparking up his own cigarette. He took a drag and exhaled a small circular ring into the wind.

Ryan shrugged, "She wants to talk."

"When?"

"Tonight."

"Well that's good. It will give you both a chance to discuss what you really want to do and how best to move on."

"I don't want to talk to her. Not yet. I need time to process this in my head, you know?"

"I get that."

"Come out with me tonight."

"Man, I can't. I'm seeing Sue."

"You can see her any day. I've just found out I'm going to be a dad. If I stick this out, you won't see me for months. I'll be knee deep in shitty nappies. We need to make the most of this time together. Phone your woman, tell her you have plans. Come on, I need to go out and get drunk."

"You should talk to Jema. You need to sort this."

"It's a fucking baby. It's not going anywhere. Come on, I need this. Please. Come out with me. Just for a couple of drinks and then I'll go and meet her. I promise."

Jim laughed, "Fine. Okay. Just a couple."

The long-term friends both stood there a moment in the afternoon sunshine, finishing their cigarettes in silence. Both were laughing to themselves; they both knew that going out for a drink never resulted in 'a couple'. Whenever they went out it turned into a full on, heavy night. Ryan didn't care though. He needed this time, just one night, to go out and unwind before facing up to his responsibilities. He figured it wouldn't do any harm.

It was only one night. Jema would understand.

#

I had twisted my body round so that my two feet were pressed against the cold brick wall of my prison. The cuff was pulling uncomfortably at my wrist but I had to ignore the pain if I were to stand any chance of breaking free. The plan was simple: gripping the pipe I was restrained to, I was going to push hard against the wall with my feet. By doing so, I hoped to pull the pipe away from the wall thus enabling me to slide my cuff over the top and away from it. In my head it worked perfectly but in reality there wasn't enough movement to make it very easy and I felt as though my arm were about to pop right out of my socket. Regardless, I closed my eyes, and pushed away from the wall with all of the strength I could muster. The metal pipe creaked but didn't budge. I screamed as I tried for a second time, and then a third. Nothing. I released the pipe and - quickly as I could - twisted round again so I was in the more comfortable position of having my back to the wall. *Fuck.*

"This is your fault," I told myself. "You deserve this."

In my head I did deserve this. I was being punished although I had yet to find out by whom. I should have gone straight home. I should have gone straight home and had it out with Jema; thrashed out what we were going to do with regards to our future and our baby's future.

"You're a selfish prick, that's what you are." I berated myself further. "Reap what you sow." I banged my head back against the wall in frustration. "You're a selfish prick and now you're going to die here."

Footsteps in what I presumed to be a corridor beyond the closed door caused me to jump. I had gotten used to not hearing anyone so close to me; gotten used to the fact I was alone, more or less. I froze as I realised they'd stopped beyond the door. I was too scared to call out. The pessimistic part of my brain screaming at me that it isn't someone who has come to help me. My usual negative outlook on life warning me it's the person who put me here in the first place; come to check up on me, make sure I'm being a good little prisoner.

Adrenaline surged through my veins as the door handle turned slowly, creaking as it did so from where it hadn't been oiled for as many years as this building had no doubt stood. Please go away, please go away, please go away.

It might be help?

It's not help.

Slowly the door creaked open. The corridor outside was just as dark as this room now was and I couldn't make out who was standing there. Just the shape. The large shape.

Fuck me.

"Hello? Who's there?" I asked.

They mimicked me, "Hello? Who's there?" the voice was deep yet raspy with something infantile about it.

"Look - I think there's been a misunderstanding..."

"Look," they repeated, "I think there's been a misunderstanding."

"Why are you doing this?"

"Why are you doing this?"

"Please - stop it!" I begged.

"Please - stop it!"

I stopped speaking. I just sat there watching whoever it was. What did they want? They weren't coming into the room. They weren't doing anything other than standing there, in darkness, watching me. My heart was beating so damned fast it felt as though it were going to pop through my rib-cage and a sickness swirled in my gut. Who the fuck is this? It's Jim. Yes. Jim. This is just a practical joke. Like jokes are played on grooms, before they get married - this must be something similar to people expecting to be a father; a sick joke just to mess with their heads. Yes. That has to be it.

Keep telling yourself that.

"Did Jim put you up to this?" the size of the man standing there suggested it wasn't Jim. This person - whoever it was - must be near seven foot at least.

"Did Jim put you up to this?" the person repeated before slowly shaking his head from side to side as though answering the question he'd just echoed.

"Then who?"

"Then who?"

I wasn't sure whether I shouted from anger, fear, frustration, or a mixture of both but - as soon as I did so - I regretted it, "WHO THE FUCK ARE YOU?!"

The man screamed, raising his hands to his ears. I screamed too, fearful of what was coming next. It turned and ran from the doorway, leaving the door open. I could do nothing but sit there as I heard the hulk's footsteps grow fainter as they disappeared down the corridor. My heart skipped another beat as a door slammed somewhere within the building. As my heart started to return to a healthier rhythm, classical music started echoing through the rooms; playing loudly somewhere in the building.

I screamed out once more, hoping my voice would be heard over the classical music, "GET BACK HERE!" I froze, waiting for a response of some description. That damned music. I know that song, what the hell was it? "HELLO?!"

Be patient, call out when the music stops.

At least I know I'm not alone. That man, that thing, he is the reason why I am here undoubtedly but he is also the key to me getting out of here too. I just need to win his trust. If I can do that, he might undo this cuff.

Trust? You mean how Jema trusted you?

MONSTER

2.

Ryan's mobile phone was resting on the bar in front of
where he was sitting with Jim. The phone was vibrating
violently every few minutes, disturbing the remaining
beer in the pint-glass next to it; a small ripple running
across the top of the golden liquid. Even though the
phone was on vibrate, and had been since he first took
the call from Jema with news of the pregnancy, it was
still hard to ignore it. Both he and Jim were looking at it.

"You should answer it," said Jim. He was all up for
coming out for a drink with his friend but - at the end of
the day - he knew Ryan had to sort things out with Jema.
Leaving her hanging, as he was now, was an asshole
move and she needed to be told one way or the other as
to what his feelings were about impending fatherhood.

"You're just trying to get out of buying your round,"
Ryan said. He lifted his pint glass from the bar and
drained the remnants before putting the glass down again
with a heavy thud. "I seem to remember paying for the
most drinks last time too," he said. He wasn't mistaken.
He was always the first to come into the pub, he was
always the first to the bar, he was always the first to get
in the rounds and Jim, well he was always first to the
toilet and first to say he had to stagger home after
drinking too much. A decision he made when it was
always his round.

The phone stopped buzzing.

"Okay then, how about this: you call her back whilst I
get the drinks in? At least let her know where you are.
You're being a dick," Jim said. He too finished his drink.
He waved the barman over to give him his order, "Two
more, please."

"I'm being a dick? What about her?"

26

"What about her?"

"She's pregnant! She's trying to trap me in a relationship! You don't think she is being a dick?"

"You don't even know she is doing that. Regardless, if that is or isn't what she is doing, I guarantee she will be at home shitting herself right now."

"Maybe that's what she deserves? Let her stew it out a little. Let her know that I'm in charge."

Jim looked at his friend and shook his head in disbelief. He couldn't believe what he was hearing. He realised Ryan was just scared about the prospect of being a father but, even so, he was - as previously mentioned - being 'a dick'. The barman handed over two fresh pints and took away the other empty glasses, putting them in the small dishwashing machine just out of sight.

"Call her," Jim said.

"I'm not ready to," Ryan countered. "I'm not nearly pissed enough."

"What are you so scared of?" Jim asked.

Now it was Ryan who was looking at him in disbelief, "Are you being serious?"

"I am, yes. What is the problem? What are you so scared of?"

"She is pregnant."

"I know."

"With my baby."

"Yes."

"My baby? You think I am ready to be a father?"

"Why the hell not? It could be great."

"And it could be terrible!"

"Do you love her?"

"What?"

Jim repeated his question, "Do you love Jema?"

"Yes." There was no hesitation.

"And she clearly loves you. So what's the problem?"

"I just expected to be married first before we had any children. I just thought…"

"Sometimes life doesn't work like that and you have to work with what you get. She's pregnant, it's your baby - now you just need to decide whether you want to stay by her side and help raise the baby. Hell, you could even get a quick wedding in before the baby is due!" Jim said.

Ryan snorted through his nose, "A wedding? I can barely afford my flat and the bills."

"You move her in. Share the costs." He shook his head when he realised he was getting carried away with the little details. The little details were something Jema and Ryan could sort out between themselves during their chat. At the moment it was more important Ryan stopped making her wait and called her. "Just fucking call her, man."

"Fine. Whatever." Ryan picked the phone up and clicked on the missed call button. It was twenty past eight and he'd already missed seventeen calls according to the screen that loaded up. He dialled her number by clicking on her name and held the phone to his ear as he waited for the line to connect. Jim took a sip of his fresh pint and watched with anticipation; he was genuinely excited for his friend. He'd been with Sue for a few years now and - secretly - he was dying to have children of his own. Like Ryan, the pair weren't married. There hadn't even been any discussions about marriage. It was something Sue wanted as she mentioned it most months but, the more she talked about it, the less Jim felt inclined to pop the question. In conversations with Ryan about it, in the past and - funnily enough - at the same bar stools, he said it felt wrong to ask the question so close to her talking about it. He worried that she'd think it was her idea. He wanted it to be his idea. An idea which took her by surprise when he did finally ask for her hand in marriage. But first she had to stop going on about it.

"It's me," Ryan said as Jema answered the call.

Jim strained to listen to the conversation despite knowing it to be rude.

"Where are you? I'm at your flat as discussed," Jema's voice crackled down the other end of the line. Jim nudged Ryan and mouthed to him that he needed to say he was sorry.

"I'm sorry," Ryan was going to say it anyway, "I…" he took a deep breath. "I'm sorry, I'm in the pub…"

"What?"

Jim didn't need to strain to hear that.

"I'm sorry, I just needed a drink."

"You needed a drink to be able to talk to me about this?"

"You took me by surprise. I'm sorry. I… Look, go home, I'll meet you there. I'll leave now."

"Well how much have you had to drink?"

"A couple, I'm fine. Go home and I'll meet you there."

There was silence on the phone for a second. Jim sat there, a nervous expression on his face, worried that his friend had already blown it.

"I love you," Jema said quietly. Unlike Jim feeling nervous because his friend had potentially ruined his chances of raising the child with his unforgiving partner, Jema was more nervous about the fact Ryan had needed to get drunk in order to talk to her about their baby. To any woman, that wasn't a good sign. Certainly not the sign of a man ready to take his responsibilities seriously.

"I love you more," said Ryan. "I'm leaving here now."

"Okay. Bye."

The phone line clicked as Jema hung up her end of the phone. Jim breathed a sigh of relief, as did Ryan.

"I can't believe you told her you were in the pub," said Jim.

Ryan ignored him, "You'd better be right about this," he said. He stood up, ready to make his exit.

Jim laughed, "I can't believe you made me get a round in and you're not even going to drink it. You really are an asshole."

Ryan shrugged, "I was happy to stay here drinking; you're the one who talked me into having this conversation. Wish me luck."

"You don't need it," said Jim - a little jealousy creeping in.

Ryan walked from the bar, leaving his friend to the two pints. Ryan knew it wouldn't be wasted, Jim would drink them. Out in the carpark he ran through the light drizzle which seemed to have come along with 'evening' and hurried over to his waiting car. He'd had a couple to drink so whilst he might have technically been over the limit - given the fact he was quite a skinny man - he still felt as though he'd be okay to drive. As he approached the driver's door, he fished in his jacket for the keys before pulling them out and letting himself in. He slammed the door shut, closing out the miserable evening rain, and slid the key in the ignition.

He caught sight of himself in the rear-view mirror. He looked like shit. Pale-faced, bags under his eyes from an afternoon stressing, and his dark hair messed up by the drizzle in that short space of time. Butterflies fluttered in his twitching stomach.

You can do this.

He fired the car up, backed out of the space he'd parked in, and pulled out of the carpark - all the time telling himself he'd be fine…

Ryan had told Jema to go home and meet him at her own place because it was closer to get to from the pub than having to go all the way to his own place. He thought it didn't seem fair to leave her standing outside, especially now he knew it was raining, whilst he made his way. At least if she were at her place, she'd be able to relax and do what she wanted to do whilst she waited - and she'd be dry. Not that she should have too much time to wait between getting there herself and seeing him show up. Hopefully he'd have timed it right to get there close to the same time. Of course it would have been easier had she had a key to Ryan's home in order to let herself in - and that is when it suddenly dawned on him:

Having a baby and she doesn't even have a key to my place. Not a baby - my baby, he corrected himself.

He shook his head as lights before him turned from amber to red, forcing him to stop. As the windscreen wipers swept across the windscreen, keeping the increasing rain at bay, he realised he wasn't shaking his head at the lights but rather his own foolishness. He couldn't believe she didn't even have a key to his home. She had his seed growing in him and yet he didn't even think - beforehand - that it would be good for her to have her own damned key. And Jim reckons he is ready for fatherhood? The more he started to think about the relationship he was in, the more he realised how backward everything was. First she was supposed to get a key, then she was supposed to move in, then they were supposed to get engaged, then married and - finally - children. Maybe one more step after that which would see a dog enter their lives? Or a cat?

What is she? Cat or a dog person?

As the lights turned from red to red,amber and then - finally – green, he started to panic that, despite dating for three months, he didn't actually know her.

#

The music stopped playing thirty minutes ago. I've been calling out since the final note played, begging the person to come back and talk to me, tell me what they wanted. But they've gone quiet. Had it not been for the fact I had seen them standing in the doorway, I'd have doubted they even existed in the first place. I'd have believed I was alone in here. My voice was croaky now from all the shouting and my throat sore and for what? I've achieved nothing. Panic started to set in as pieces from the previous night (was it the previous night) started to slip back into my conscious thoughts from wherever I'd initially lost them. I just want to know why I am here. I want to know what is going on. I want to know what I've done to deserve this - other than be an asshole boyfriend, that is. There's a million men - most likely a lot more than that - out there who are like me; some of them shirking all of their responsibilities. How do I deserve this more than them? How can I get picked out of all the people out there.

I tried to scream again but it was so feeble I doubted it would have even been heard beyond the first closed door. Tears had started to well up in my eyes, a couple of which spilled down my cold cheeks.

Cold. So damned cold.

I'm not sure what time it is. I don't appear to be wearing my watch and nor do I have my mobile phone on me anymore. Not sure whether they were confiscated or whether I'd removed them from my persons before being taken (was I even taken?). Beyond the small, cracked window on the far wall - the night is as black as death. It must be late. I know I should try and get some sleep, I should try and rest up a little. I'm so tired, even feel a little groggy from being knocked out (was I drugged?). It's obvious they're not coming back for me tonight; they've either gone to sleep in one of the other rooms or left for the night, returning to wherever they live whilst waiting for morning to - maybe - come back to me? Should I try and call out once more or save what remains of my voice for morning?

Save it. Get some rest. You're going to need it. Need to stay sharp. Need to stay focused.

It is hard to stay sharp or focused when I feel so hungry. I can't remember the last time I had anything to eat or anything - non-alcoholic - to drink. So hungry I want to throw up.

Don't. Don't waste whatever energy is left there.

I closed my eyes. I don't think I will manage to sleep, not in this position; my arm raised where it is attached to the wall and the uneven brickwork digging into my back. I'm not going to sleep. There's no chance of that.

Try.

I kept my eyes closed and wished myself to another place.

BEAST

1.

Large, clumsy fingers fiddled with a small, silver crank attached to the box in the sweaty palm of the other hand. The large shape, partially consumed by the darkness of the room, rocked excitedly where it perched on a rickety chair over in the corner. Rocking backwards and forwards, a wheezy laugh escaped deformed lips hidden beneath a mask made of stinking flesh. With each turn of the crank, more of *Ring around the Roses* played into the room, drowning out the frequent drips of water splashing the concrete floor from ripped holes in the damp ceiling of the old building. Something clicked within the dirty box and the lid flew open - pushed by a rotten severed hand attached to a spring. The large shape jumped and howled with fear before throwing the box across the room where it smashed against the far wall. In another room, down a dark, dingy corridor - someone else was also screaming. The shape suddenly rose to its full height of just over seven foot tall. It moved across the room to where the broken box laid, the severed hand now detached from the spring a few feet away. The shape changed slightly as it outstretched a large, muscular arm with a shaking hand. It picked the box up and lurched over to the severed hand, the entire time making panicked grunts as though it were a scared, yet inquisitive ape. With the severed hand in one hand and the box, with spring, in the other - it tried pushing the two components together. It released the rotting body part and screeched in frustration when it dropped to the floor, unfixed. Undeterred it collected the fallen hand once more and took both that and the musical box to the other side of the room where it - once again - pressed the two parts together with the hope that a change of position would do the trick. It released the box this time, keeping hold of the severed hand, and howled as it clattered to the floor; a cat-like hiss escaped the shape's unseen mouth when it realised the crank had sheared off too.

The shape dropped to a seated position in the darkness and started rocking backwards and forwards; releasing a pained cry as it did so. It stopped suddenly at the sound of a voice in a distant room. Someone - scared - calling out from the darkness. The person - a man - screamed out again and the shape sat up tall like an alerted meerkat. Slowly - in the darkness - the shape twisted its hidden face towards the only door in the near empty room. Another scream for someone's attention, in the distance, and the shape visibly got excited - swaying from side to side whilst making weird grunting noises from its throat. With no warning it leapt back up to its full height and stormed towards the door, pulling it open with so much excitement that the damned thing nearly flew off the rusted hinges holding it in place.

"Hello? Is there anyone there? Can you hear me? Please, I need your help!"

A little flickering light hanging from the ceiling in the corridor couldn't illuminate the whole of the shape, but it lit enough to show this wasn't an ordinary man. Around seven feet in height with a muscular body, the man stood there with an arch in his back which gave him a slight humpback in his appearance. His neck was twisted to one side, giving his head a permanent lean to the left. A little dribble of saliva hung from his unseen mouth, down his chin, and stained boiler suit. Even had the light been better and afforded more visibility - his face would have remained a mystery as it was buried under a mask made of flesh torn from the features of what was once another man. The mask further gave the impression that this was more monster than man.

"Hello?" the voice called out from further down the corridor.

The monster swayed from side to side in the corridor, clearly excited by the sounds of another person; each time hitting his shoulders against the walls - which were too narrow for someone of his structure.

"Is anyone there?"

He started to run down the corridor; a run unlike any other human. Two steps forward before falling to the floor and running for another two steps on all fours - like a charging gorilla - before back up to two legs again for another couple of paces. Given the beast's size, it didn't take long to reach the source of the voice. It stopped by the door and sniffed the air. Slowly it raised its hand to the door and gave the handle a slight twist - causing the rusted metal workings of the handle to creak and groan. It pushed the door open and just stood there, looking at the man within the room; a stranger, sitting against the far wall - a handcuff restraining him to one of the many pipes running through the building.

"Hello?" the man called out. "Who's there?"

The beast mimicked him in a deep raspy, yet infantile, tone, "Hello? Who's there?"

"Look - I think there's been a misunderstanding..."

"Look, I think there's been a misunderstanding."

The man started getting frustrated, "Why are you doing this?"

Underneath the mask, the man in the room couldn't see the look of bemusement on the creature's face; bemusement and amusement. "Why are you doing this?"

"Please - stop it!" the man begged, clearly nervous of his situation.

"Please - stop it!"

They both fell into a silence. The man pulled at the cuff keeping him on the wall once more. It was obvious he wasn't going anywhere. The beast, watching, tilted his head - curious at the man's behaviour. The man momentarily seemed to calm down.

"Did Jim put you up to this?" the man asked.

"Did Jim put you up to this?" the beast slowly shook his head from side to side though he wasn't aware of the question being asked.

"Then who?"

"Then who?"

The man lashed out in the beast's direction with a foot as he screamed, "WHO THE FUCK ARE YOU?"

The beast screamed out loud and raised his hands to his ears; his own scream causing the man to scream too. Without a further word, or warning, the beast turned and ran from the room - back down the corridor using the similar pattern from before: two steps forward on two feet, a couple of paces on all four, back to two feet - all the way down the length of the dingy corridor towards a room at the far end. Now on two feet, it gave a check over its shoulder before disappearing into the room, slamming the door behind it.

Unlike the other two rooms this one at least looked a little lived-in. There was a bed in the far corner of the room with a dirty mattress on top - no sheets in sight. A mannequin's head sat on a table along the wall with the door and a rug was in the middle of the floor as though in desperate attempt to give it a homely feel. Perhaps it if weren't made from stretched skin? The beast fell onto the bed and curled into a little ball. A second later and it rolled to the edge of the mattress - not that there was far to roll - and pulled an old gramophone from underneath where it lay. A record was sitting on the machine already, waiting to be played. With oversized, clumsy fingers - the beast set the record spinning.

Ring-a-ring-a-roses…

The beast returned to its previous position - curled into a ball upon the heavily-stained mattress; a strained, whimpering noise coming from beneath the stinking mask. He didn't like the shouting. It made him uncomfortable, nervous even. It reminded him of *them*. As the music continued to play, filling both the room and his senses, he closed his eyes and slowly allowed himself to relax. A couple of minutes later and it had been lulled to sleep by the sounds of the music. The record stopped at the end of the song, but continued to spin - filling the room with a soft hum. The beast didn't wake until the morning.

#

There were no clocks on the wall to determine the time but beyond the small window, on the wall opposite the monster's bed, a shimmer of light spilled into the room. Eyes were closed behind the man-made mask. A puddle of dribble trickled from beneath the jaw-line of the same mask, pooling in a sticky mess of yellow on the already tainted pillow. A rasping, wheezing noise escaped into the room as the monster behind the mask struggled for air as he slept - dreaming dreams of whatever monsters dream. The monster awoke with a sudden fright as a scream filled the building; not one of fear but one of pain. In a split second it was out of its bed and across the room with a lurch. It ripped the door open and turned into the corridor where it froze on the spot; listening, waiting. The building was silent with the exception of a steady gust of wind blowing in from one of the many cracks in the brickwork. The beast stood there a moment longer before mimicking the pained scream that had stirred him from his sleep. A door slammed from within the building. The monster charged towards the room where he'd seen the stranger the night before. He stopped outside of the door. It was closed. He twisted his neck to the side as he took a moment to remember whether he'd closed it the previous night. He hadn't. The beast took a step back and looked from side to side. No one else around to close it. Slowly, he raised his right hand and twisted the handle. A gentle push and the door opened. There - hanging on the wall by a silver handcuff - was an arm. Just an arm, swinging backwards and forwards from the momentum used to hack it away from body; blood dripping onto the floor.

The beast screamed out in a lonely rage.

SHAW / BRAY

MONSTER

MATT SHAW

&

MICHAEL BRAY

SHAW / BRAY

MONSTER

PART ONE

SHAW / BRAY

CHAPTER ONE

The clock had been stuck at 10:42am forever, or at least that's how it felt. Thirty-five year old Christina Cooper sighed and turned away from the mocking timepiece, hoping to find something else to distract her. She stared out of the window, the forecourt of the gas station as deserted as it always was. Long yellow grass surrounded the four pump station, which sat pretty much as far from civilisation as it was possible to get, or at least it felt that way. During summer months, the grass was nice to look at from the counter where she seemed to spend all her time. It would catch the sunlight, shimmering and swaying and looking almost like corn. When it was raining like today though, there was nothing beautiful about it. The rain made it look somehow ugly and filled the gas station with a funny, earthy smell, which was hard to get rid of no matter how much air freshener she sprayed. She glanced at the clock.

10:44am

She turned to the magazine rack, searching for something she hadn't already read and discovered nothing. Her eyes then went to the shelves filled with treats and snacks, which she also immediately dismissed. She decided she was miserable enough with the mundaneness of her life and job that she didn't want to compound it further by eating the entire stock of chocolate in the building. Eyes to clock.

Still 10:44am

Something caught her eye - a car making its way over the crest on the horizon, a rooster tail of dust kicked up behind it. As much as it hardly filled her with joy, at least a potential customer might help to pass a little time, that was if they even stopped at all. She watched as it grew closer. It was a convertible in red. Its driver a silver haired business man wearing ridiculous sunglasses despite the rain and general gloom of the day. He did indeed require fuel, and drove his penis extension of a car right up to pump two. She sighed. He was playing music far too loud that he was much too old to be listening to. She watched as he got out of the car, wrinkling his nose.

Shitty grass smell, she thought to herself as she watched him go through the process of refueling. She had worked there for long enough (another can of worms she didn't particularly want to open) to usually predict how a given customer would pay for their purchase. Younger groups, who would be looking to buy some food for their journey, would invariably come into the station to pay directly, usually snickering at the shitty little backwards place where she earned her living. Others however, like Mr. Dick on Wheels out in the carpark, were pump payers. Too busy to want to deal with anything resembling human interaction, they were looking to pay and go on to whichever business meeting, seminar, or affair with the other woman to waste time making small talk. She watched him and knew she was going to do it. She had a game, something to help her pass the time. It was petty and more than a little childish, but as it was hers and hers alone, and so she felt no guilt. Whenever customers would come, be it to pay at the pump or in person, she would create profiles for them - usually morbid ones. Her current fascination was with serial killers, more specifically the spate of recent disappearances of people in the area. The causal interest she had started with had grown into obsession, and the more she read on the subject, the more she wanted to learn. It was a vicious cycle. People were likening it to a modern day Jack the Ripper case. No evidence, no clues. No witnesses. It was a mystery and one she was hungry for more information on. She normally brought her notebook with her. Sometimes to doodle in, sometimes to make notes on the case as she scoured the internet for information on the disappearances, looking for any new information that might shed some light on it. She focused back on her customer, who as predicted was fishing out his wallet ready to pay at the pump. She assessed him, building up a back story, giving him a character. She saw him as a Julian, or an Alex, or maybe one of those pretentious dicks who only gave people their second name.

Yes.

It would be something slick, powerful, a name that screamed arrogance.

Benedict.

Or maybe Mayweather.

She smiled, enjoying her secret game.

Mayweather, she had decided, was a powerful Wall Street trader. Trophy wife. Semi-serious gambling addiction. By night, he was the Moonlight Slasher. Luring women back to his apartment using his money, power, and confidence, then cutting them to pieces in a demented half tribute to Christian Bale's Nicholas Bateman character from American Psycho.

Her grin broadened, and she pushed a lock of brown hair behind her ear.

10:49am

Not bad. She glanced at her phone, hoping Greg had been in touch, but the display was blank. No message, no notifications. She sighed, glancing back to the window to see the Moonlight Slasher spinning his wheels as he fishtailed away from the forecourt, throwing stones and gravel up behind the car as he went on his way to wherever he was headed.

"Dickhead." She muttered under her breath.

She looked at the clock.

10:50am. It was going to be a long day.

#

Thursday came and was just as mundane as the Wednesday had been. At least there had been a steadier stream of customers coming through the door, making the need to clock watch a little less of a priority. For every up there was a down, and today it came in the form of the store manager: a fat, greasy, balding man by the name of Nizoy. He was eastern European, and had come over from the Ukraine in order to start a new life. As a man he was cruel and unfriendly, his instructions delivered in barks and grunts. As a boss he was worse and had made a habit of taking little interest in how the store was run until head office would complain; after which he would gladly throw his employees under the wheels of the bus in order to save his own skin. Christina was grateful he was locked up in his office, supposedly doing paperwork. Even better, she wasn't alone in the store for once. Her friend, Jessie, had come in to keep her company. Although she was nine years younger, they still shared a lot of common interests, including a love of the macabre. Where Christina was naturally pretty in the sense that she wore little makeup or felt no need to make crazy fashion statements to get noticed, Jessie was the opposite. Her hair seemed to change colour weekly (today she was sporting red and purple streaks in the front). Underneath all the rebellion, she was a sweet girl who was stuck in a cycle of feeling obliged to keep her outlandish look.

"It's like a morgue in here," Jessie said as she leaned on the counter, staring out at the empty forecourt.

"Welcome to my world," Christina muttered as she checked her phone to see if Greg had been in touch. She had a text from him asking her to bring in some eggs and milk when she came home. She thought about replying, then set her phone back on the shelf under the counter. "I need to get out of here, Jessie. I'm wasting my life doing this."

"So leave. Walk out. Fuck this place."

"I can't just go. I have responsibilities, bills to pay...."

"That sounds like an excuse to me," Jessie countered, grabbing a chocolate bar from the counter and opening it.

"Jessie, Nizoy is in his office!" she whispered.

"I don't give a fuck; the fat prick can come out and tell me to stop if he wants to," Jessie said, enjoying her friend's discomfort as she said it louder than she had to. She took a huge bite of the chocolate bar.

"Come on, cut it out," Christina said, now unable to help grinning herself.

"Seriously though," Jessie said, handing over the bar which Christina tossed into the bin. "Why do you insist on wasting your time working here? You've been here for, what, how long now?"

"Six years," she said with a sigh.

"Exactly. We both know you pretty much do everything around here too. Have you ever been offered a promotion? A pay rise?"

"No, but-"

"No buts, Chris. You're better than this place. You could be earning an extra seven grand a year somewhere else doing the same job fat boy in the office is doing, but actually doing it right."

"I don't know; I just feel like…. I have to stay here to keep the place running."

Jessie looked around the deserted space. "Running? This place is dying a slow death, and if you're not careful, it will take you with it."

"Please, Jess, I know you're just trying to help, but please just drop it, okay?"

"I'm sorry, I just…" Jessie sighed and shrugged her petite shoulder. "I hate seeing you taken advantage of like this, you know?"

"I know, I just….It's complicated right now."

Jessie lowered her head, stared at the counter, then looked out of the window.

"Hey check it out; you might actually have a customer." Jessie said, stifling a yawn and checking her watch.

Christina looked out of the window, watching the grubby white van as it approached. They watched as it pulled up to the pump. Its driver, a skinny, frail looking man, climbed carefully out, paused to catch his breath, and then walked to the pump. As he picked it up, he looked like he was about to drop it, but then grabbed it at the second attempt.

Pump payer. Christina thought, then turned back to her phone, intending to reply to Greg.

"Go on," Jessie said, flashing a wide grin. "Profile them. Tell me their story."

"No, I really don't feel like it." She replied, already thinking of scenarios in her head.

"Come on, Chris. Get that imagination of yours going. Tell me about the white van guy."

"Alright," She said, turning to look out of the window. Jessie followed her gaze.

"He's a divorcee, no wait, a widower." She said, making it up as she went. "No kids, no family who still speak to him. He's one of those hoarders. Newspapers piled to the ceiling, all sorts of broken shit he hasn't thrown away all over the house, which stinks of piss, booze, and stale farts."

She stared at the man, then at his van, which was way overdue to be washed.

"At night, he goes out in the van. Cruising the streets, maybe down in the red light district. He takes his time, looking for the right kind of prostitute. He likes them young, fresh faced. Younger the better. When he finds her he'll pay up, scrambling around for change, just about having enough to cover the price. He drives her somewhere dark, secluded; only, when it gets down to it, he can't get it up. He sits there, trying to beat some life into himself, trying to will it to work. All the time, the prostitute, too young to know the rules properly, snickers and laughs at him - the old man who can't get it up even for someone as young and tight as her. He gets angry, lashes out. She might see it too late, a flicker maybe in his eyes which reminds her how dangerous a profession she's chosen."

She pauses for a moment, building the story, fleshing it out. "He might look weak," She says, continuing on. "But when that anger strikes, when that rage at his inability to be a man comes, he finds strength. An inner power. He lunges, grabbing her by the throat, maybe slamming her head off the dashboard to silence the screams. She's unconscious, maybe bloody-nosed, but alive. That's when he starts to feel it, that feeling in his stomach, that stirring in his groin. He knows just what to do. He drives back to his house, enjoying the anticipation, keeping a close eye on her. She might try to wake up, and if she does he just slams her head right back into the dashboard. He gets home, but he doesn't want his neighbour to see, so he tosses her into the back of the van, climbing in after her. He climbs on top of her, but he's not quite able to perform."

She pauses, dimly aware that Jessie is watching her, absolutely mesmerised.

"That rage comes again, bubbling up in his stomach," She says quietly. "He knows he doesn't have to restrain it anymore, so he lets it come, lets it grow and fill his veins, fill his nerve endings, setting them on fire. He grabs her neck, but not until she's awake. He wants her to experience this. He wants her to know what she's caused. He squeezes, teeth clenched, sweat pouring out of him. Now he's feeling it, now he's getting aroused. He times it so that he shoots his load just as she dies, moaning as he fires it into his filthy underwear. Later, when his neighbours will be asleep, he'll go out again, looking for somewhere quiet to dump the body, maybe in a quarry or out in the woods somewhere. Maybe that's where he's going right now, maybe he has some-"

"Excuse me!"

Thy both turned - unaware that someone had come into the shop. She had obviously overheard the entire conversation, and Christina lowered her head, embarrassed. Jessie simply snorted and stared the woman out.

She was around seventy, her hair short and silver. Her skin was almost olive and lined deeply. Her mouth was cruel and puckered, the deep lines in her skin telling the story of her age in the same way the rings on a tree would. She glared at them, eyes harsh, lips pursed. She slammed the carton of milk down on the counter.

"When you're ready." She said.

"Of course, sorry," Christina muttered, ringing the purchase through the till. "Can I get you anything else?"

"No," the woman said, tossing a ten on the counter. "Not right now."

Christina gave the woman her change. For a moment she stood there, staring at the two of them. Then walked away, pushed through the door, and walked across the forecourt. The two women watched as she stopped by the white van and started talking to the man, gesticulating towards the gas station.

"Are you fucking kidding me?" Jessie said, breaking into a chuckle. "That must be the guy's wife. No wonder she was so pissed off. You just compared him to Jack the Ripper."

"Shit, shit, shit. I hope she doesn't complain to Nizoy. That's all I need."

"Not much you can do now," Jessie said, watching as the woman got into the passenger seat of the van and glared across at the building as her husband duly paid at the pump. He followed her lead, clambering into the driver's side, a task which seemed to take an extraordinary effort. The van rolled around the pumps, slowly going past the window to the gas station; the man and woman at the wheel both glared through the window before driving away back the way they had come, sunlight glittering off the wing mirrors as it went.

"That was brilliant," Jessie said, nudging her friend's shoulder. "Really made my day."

Christina gave a non-committal grunt as she watched the vehicle disappear over the crest of the road and out of sight. She sighed. As far as working weeks went, she decided this one was turning out to be pretty shitty.

#

She couldn't sleep. She glanced across at Greg, who lay on his side, the rhythmic sounds of undisturbed sleep of a man without troubles. Unlike her, he was happy and secure in his job. Worse was that he thought she was too, so never questioned it. She longed to talk to him about it, and knew that if she did he would be a great listener like he always was. The trouble was, she didn't want to admit her unhappiness, fearing it would have a house of cards effect on their relationship. She half considered waking him up, explaining how she was feeling, but knew she wouldn't. It wasn't fair. Instead, she got out of bed, glancing at the clock and realising that those things had started to rule both her nights and her days.

2:44am

She was grateful she had the late shift next day, so at least she wouldn't have to face the long day exhausted. She crossed the room, feet padding on the polished floorboards. She let herself out of the bedroom, crossed the hall, and gently opened the bedroom door opposite.

Like her father, their thirteen year old daughter Courtney was deep in trouble free sleep. Christina felt better for seeing her, even if she wasn't awake. Her family unit was the only thing keeping her going, and she couldn't imagine not having them around. She closed the door and went downstairs. She considered making coffee, then thought better of it. If she was struggling to sleep, the last thing she needed was caffeine in her system further keeping her awake. Instead, she went into the living room, easily navigating it in the dark. She flicked on one of the lamps by the sofa and powered up her laptop, then grabbed her pen and notebook.

She did the usual routine. Quick email check, a quick scan of Facebook and Twitter to see if anyone else was burning the midnight oil. Eventually, she opened her web browser and went to the bookmarks.

Her interest in the recent spate of disappearances had grown into obsession. She had read every article she could find, every forum, weeded out fact from fiction in an effort to see if she could discover the missing piece of the puzzle that might lead to them being solved. She was aware of course, that as the police couldn't find anything, her chances were slim, but she also reasoned that they would likely have other cases to be working on at the same time, whereas she could devote as much time as she needed to it. Although she knew it all intimately, she pulled up the information, reading through it again, hoping something jumped out at her. The first article dated back to 1991. She opened it up, reading and taking in information she already knew.

HUNT FOR MISSING STUDENT CONTINUES

August 4th 1991
Police admitted last night to having no leads following the disappearance of college student Victor Horrowitz last night, and have once again appealed to the public for any information which may assist with their enquiries. Horrowitz (19) was last seen leaving a party to celebrate a friend's graduation. After separating form friends a little after midnight, he failed to return home. Despite an in-depth search and appeals for witnesses, no information as to his whereabouts has come to light. The Indiana State Police Department have asked that anyone with information about Horrowitz or who was with him at the party to get in touch immediately on (765) 567-2125

She turned to the next article, this one featuring a photograph of the victim - a young girl with a bright smile and long blonde hair.

FEARS MOUNT FOR MISSING TEEN

August 9th 1991
Fears are mounting for an Indiana teen who
disappeared on her way back from visiting friends last
night, prompting fears that a serial kidnapper might be
on the loose. Just days after appeals to locate another
missing student, Victor Horrowitz, eighteen year old
Nina Rodgers has also seemingly disappeared without
trace. Miss Rodgers was walking home after visiting a
friend who lived ten minutes away from her home.
Despite this, Miss Rodgers never arrived. Her Friends
confirmed to police that neither of them had been
drinking, and Miss Rodgers wasn't the type of person to
go somewhere without telling her family. Police have
again appealed for any information from anyone who
may know or have seen Miss Rodgers last night.

No matter how often she read them, the reports always
disturbed her. Something in her gut resonated with the
reports, perhaps fears for her own daughter who would
soon be grown up and going out with friends without
supervision. Not particularly wanting to go down that
train of thought, she read on. The next occurrence came
a year later almost to the day.

MAJOR HUNT UNDERWAY FOR MISSING CHILD

August 3rd 1992

Extra officers were drafted in yesterday to assist in the
search for a ten year old girl who was snatched during a
visit to a local shop just three hundred meters from her
home. An eye witness says the girl was bundled into a

blue van with a sliding side door, however due to the angle of the witness, the identity or description of the driver remains a mystery. A twenty thousand dollar reward has been issued for her safe return. Anyone with information should contact the Indiana Police Department immediately and ask to speak to detective Johnston.

The pattern went on, year on year. Always around the start of August. Sometimes just one would be taken, on other occasions three or more. Race, age, or sex didn't seem to make a difference. No bodies were ever found. It was as if they had literally disappeared off the face of the earth without explanation. Of course, the assumption that they were dead was easy. Christina was interested in the reason why. She picked up her notepad, leafing back to one of the early pages she had written during what felt like an age ago. It was a list of the victims along with their ages and dates they were take which made grim reading.

Victor Horrowitz (19) August 4th 1991
Nina Rodgers (18) August 9th 1991
Abigail Greer (10) August 3rd 1992
Andy Mears (24) August 4th 1992
Glen Orson (22) August 10th 1993
Jane Keller (40) August 5th 1994
Jose Campo (34) August 7th 1994
Milly Anderson (7) August 9th 1995
Joseph Kanu (14) August 10th 1996

There was then an inexplicable gap. It seemed as if whoever was responsible either deliberately stopped or had other reasons not to continue. The period of disappearances, which she referred to as phase two, picked up again in the summer of 2004. She read on.

Joan Franks (31) July 30th 2004
Eileen Kruger (26) August 2 2004

She paused again. Nothing between 05 and 09, then like clockwork it started again.

John Dean (20) August 3rd 2010
Lucy Oakre (22) August 5th 2010
Pamela Steen (15) August 13th 2011
Dan jones (32) August 1st 2011
Claire Alcock August 7th 2012

Then nothing. No evidence. No bodies found. Nothing at all since then. She glanced at the clock on her desktop, her stomach tightening a little.
2:53am
01/08/14

August.

She thought of her daughter, sleeping in her bed, and tried to imagine how it would be to lose her. To have her join the list of people she had no doubt were dead. Anxiety surged through her, a borderline panic attack. She felt so isolated, so alone and without help. She knew of course it was ridiculous to think anything was going to happen to her or her family, but even so it still troubled her. She looked around the shadow draped room, listening to the house. It was big and old, and like all old houses, it made noises. Creaks and groans as it shifted on old foundations which certainly didn't help her nerves. She decided that perhaps now wasn't the time to be reading about such morbid things, especially if she intended on ever getting any sleep. With a sigh, she powered off the laptop and set it and her notepad on the seat beside her. With nothing else for it, she went back to bed; hoping sleep would come without really believing it would. She lay in the dark, listening to the wind rattle the old house, one arm behind her head. Against all odds she drifted into sleep, vague dreams of disembodied arms reaching out of the night to snatch her into the abyss.

CHAPTER TWO

She arrived at work just after six thirty, ready for night shift. If the days were slow, the night shift in comparison was still. She would be lucky to get more than a couple of customers all night. The thought of another night spent clockwatching and waiting for the misery of her shift to end was unappealing on its own, even without thinking about her research. She supposed part of her discomfort was due to the time of year. It was natural to be on edge when she knew so much about it. Knowing there was nothing else she could do about it, she got out of her car and walked into the mundane familiarity of the gas station.

"You're early," Abul said from behind the counter, greeting her with a warm grin.

He had only worked at the gas station for a couple of months, and so hadn't let the utter misery of being stuck in such a boring job get to him yet.

"I guess I just can't get enough of the place," she sighed as she joined him behind the counter.

Abul grinned and pushed his glasses back up his face. "Yeah right. You look thrilled to be here."

He exited the counter as she took his place. She put her phone on charge and set it under the counter, then glanced around the empty room.

"How's it been tonight?" she asked.

"Quiet again. You're in for a quiet one I think." He said as he grabbed his bag. He crossed the room towards the door, then stopped. "Oh, don't forget you're covering my shift tomorrow night."

"I remember," she sighed. "Two consecutive night shifts. Oh joy."

Abul grinned. "I appreciate it. I have this presentation to finish for my course. I owe you one."

"Damn right you do," she replied. "I'll hold you to it too."

"Oh, before I forget, there was someone in here asking after you earlier."

"After me?" She said, feeling a flicker of discomfort. "Who was it?"

"I don't know."

"What did they look like?"

"I don't know, they didn't speak to me. Nizoy spoke to them. He's sent me to the wholesalers."

She shook her head. "You do know he's not supposed to send us there? He's meant to go himself."

"I know but I'm still on probation here. I didn't really have a choice."

She frowned, unsure why she felt so uncomfortable. "Did they leave a message?"

Abul shrugged. "Not that I know of. Probably best if you talk to Nizoy about it tomorrow."

"Yeah, I'll do that," she said, mind already wandering. "Thanks Abul."

"Anytime. Don't forget about tomorrow. I gotta run, take it easy Christina."

"Yeah, you too." She muttered as she was left alone. She watched Abul go, shoulders hunched as he disappeared into the sunset. For the first time in a long time, she was afraid of the coming night.

#

Her irrational fear turned out to be just that. Nothing unusual came with the night, and there were no strange occurrences. She had only served two customers all night, three if she counted the young woman who had stopped to ask for directions. She locked up as per the usual routine - turning out lights, setting the alarm, ensuring the mesh security grills were in place over the windows. She stood by the door, looking out into the pitch dark, the soft glow of city streets nothing more than an orange haze on the horizon. She was in what she called countryside dark. Here, there were no streetlights. She could see the stars in their brilliance, thousands of tiny diamonds which made her appreciate just how small and insignificant she was. Another thought crept into her mind, oozing over the positivity. One which told her such isolation would be ideal for somebody out looking to snatch a person without being seen. She looked out into the long yellow grasses which hissed in the wind. Under the moonlight they looked sickly and pale. She imagined someone crouching out there, perhaps staring at her as she stood there like a deer in the headlights, shop keys in hand, miles from civilisation.

That was all it took to spur her on. She walked to her car, desperate not to do the tired old cliché of dropping her keys as some unnamed menace approached from the shadows. She forced herself to remain calm as she unlocked the car and got in, locking the doors behind her. She glanced around at the fields, watching for any sign of movement, then when there were none, chastised herself for reading too much horror and letting it pollute her rationale.

Feeling foolish, she started the engine and drove away, relieved to be heading back to civilisation. Twice on the way home, that macabre part of her brain tried to convince her she was being followed, and twice she dismissed it as stupid and nothing more than her overactive imagination. She arrived home, relieved to see the lights in the lounge on and inviting. She walked towards the door, able to see Greg through the window, feet up on the sofa as he watched television. She relaxed, and chastised herself again for watching too many movies and reading too many books. Real life was, thankfully, different and although there were monsters out there, for the majority of people their lives were never touched by them. She went in the house and locked the door behind her. After all, she reasoned, you could never be too careful.

CHAPTER THREE

She woke late the next morning, or at least late in comparison to her normal 6am alarm call. She glanced over to Greg's side of the bed, finding him to be missing, covers thrown back. The clock read 7:14. She bolted out of bed, pulled on her dressing gown, and raced downstairs, intending to try and do all the before school run prep in less than half the normal time. She entered the kitchen, unable to help but smile.

Greg had handled everything. Breakfast was made, and both he and Courtney were eating toast.

"I overslept," she mumbled.

"By design," Greg replied, smiling at her. "You looked exhausted last night. I thought I'd take the weight off a little so I turned off your alarm."

"You didn't have to do that," She said, loving him for it all the same.

"Shut up and sit down. There is coffee in the pot and toast on the table." He replied, winking at her over his newspaper.

She returned his smile and sat opposite him, grateful to have him there to support her. Courtney as usual had her head buried in her phone, no doubt chatting to her friends. Christina poured herself a coffee, enjoying not having to run around like a crazy woman for a while.

"Oh, you have mail too. It's there on the side," Greg said, nodding towards the counter behind her. She reached over and picked up the modest stack of letters addressed to her. Credit card bills. Water bill reminder. Junk mail. She hesitated at the plain white envelope at the bottom of the stack. It had no name, no address. The envelope was grubby and dog eared. She glanced towards Greg, wondering if she should ask his opinion or not, but he was reading his paper and she didn't want to bother him with something so silly. She turned her attention back to the envelope and opened it. Inside was a faded blue birthday invite. On the front was a white birthday cake with the words 'You are invited' in red bubble text at the top. Underneath, where the host would typically write the date and venue details, was just a single sentence scrawled across it in a spiky handwriting.

Do you want to know the truth?

Cold crept out of her gut, which felt like it had tightened.

"Greg, look at this," she said, handing the invite to him across the table.

"What is it?" he said, not taking it from her.

"I don't know, that's why I'm asking you to take a look," she replied, trying to hide the niggling fear. Hearing her discomfort, he folded his newspaper and set it on the table, then took the invite from her. He looked at it, frowning.

"Truth about what?" he asked.

"I don't know, it was with the mail."

"Huh, weird. Probably some stupid kids screwing around or using our letterbox as a rubbish bin, I wouldn't worry about it," he said, tossing it on the table.

She was worried about it though, something made her uncomfortable. Something didn't sit right with her, and that alone was cause for concern. Her eyes moved to Greg's paper, which was still on the table, folded open to the page he had been reading. Even upside down it was easy to read.

SUMMER ABDUCTION SPREE ANNIVERSARY LOOMS

"Can I see that?" she asked, nodding to the paper.

"Oh, yeah," Greg replied as he sipped his coffee. "I was going to save it for you. I know you have an interest in this stuff."

He handed the paper to her. It held no new information; in fact, some of the information in the piece wasn't entirely accurate. Even so, she would keep it for her scrapbook. The piece listed those abducted, and seemed to be a speculative article about if this would be the year where the sabbatical was once again broken. She glanced at Courtney, who was still lost in her phone and couldn't shake the overwhelming terror and need to protect her family.

"Can you take Christina to school this morning?" She blurted across the table.

"Mom! I can make my own way, I don't need a ride."

"I'd rather your father drops you off, if he has the time." She countered.

Greg shrugged. "I don't mind at all, but she's been going on her own for almost a year now-"

"Exactly!" Courtney cut in.

"-I don't see why the change of heart," Greg finished.

"I'd just feel better about it," was the best she could offer in way of response.

"But I'll get laughed at. Can you imagine the shame of being dropped off at school by parents?"

Christina felt bad; she could, of course, see her daughter's point. However she was more concerned with keeping her safe during this first week of August. She locked eyes with Greg, and in the way things sometimes worked with long term relationships, he locked on to the reason she was so insistent.

"Look, if your mother wants me to drop you off, that's the end of discussion."

"But Dad-"

"No buts. That's it."

"This isn't fair. None of my other friends have to be driven to school."

"I don't care about them," Christina said, slamming a hand on the table. "My concern is you. If I hear another word, you can add a grounding to the list too."

"This is unfair," She muttered, then stood, leaving the table. They listened to her stomp upstairs and slam her bedroom door.

"Jesus Christ," Christina muttered, leaning her elbows on the table and rubbing her temples. "I didn't want that to go down that way."

"Don't worry," Greg said, reaching across the table and taking her hands in his. "I get it. You always get twitchy around this time of year."

"It's weird, isn't it?"

"No, not weird," Greg said, searching for the right way to respond. "I do think you might need to step away from it for a while. I mean, if there was any evidence out there, the police would find it."

"I know, it's just….I'm interested. You know how much I like stuff like this."

"Maybe you should have been a detective," he said with a smile.

She returned the gesture, at the same time screaming inside. Wishing he knew how much she hated her life, her job. The mistakes she had made. Greg saw none of this, and thinking the discussion done, stood and straightened his tie.

"Well, I suppose I better go and tell our misery filled whirlwind upstairs that it's time to go." He walked past her and kissed her on the head. "I'll see you later."

"Yeah, I'll see you tonight," she mumbled, barely listening. She was staring at the newspaper article, then at the card. No matter how she tried she couldn't shake the feeling in her gut that something just wasn't right.

CHAPTER FOUR

With Greg at work and Courtney safely at school
(verified by attitude filled text message), Christina
walked around the house, restless and unsure what to do
with herself until work began later that night. At almost
a hundred years old, the house was too big for the three
of them, a feeling that was further amplified when she
was there alone. She didn't like the sounds it made, or
how those charming period features had a habit of
breaking, failing and costing money. She even hated
how it looked - the outside painted in pink and green. It
reminded her of a watermelon. Repainting it was just
one of a long list of things that needed to be done to put
the place in full working order, and another thing that
would just have to wait until finances could allow it. She
realised it was just like a working day. She wandered
around, waiting for the day to fade into night. By the
time she was due to head out to work, she was itching to
get going. Although she hated the job, a change of
scenery was welcome. As she left the house, she was
aware of how much she was looking forward to the
weekend. Maybe she would suggest a trip, a day out
somewhere for just the three of them to try and get away
from the house for a while. God knew they could all use
it.

#

"There she is!" Abul said, clapping his hands together
as she walked into the gas station. "My saviour arrives!"

She smiled, wishing she could muster the same kind of enthusiasm as her younger colleague. They crossed at the hatch leading to the back of the counter.

"Damn, Abul, how much aftershave are you wearing? Planning on getting lucky tonight?

"Not planning as such," Abul replied as he leaned on the other side of the counter. "But preparing for the possibility."

"Always wise. Don't miss me too much."

"We both know you're well out of my league," Abul said, slipping her a wink. "Besides, I don't want that husband of yours kicking my ass. How is Greg by the way? All good?"

"He's fine," she said, unable to help but grin.

"Glad to hear it. Courtney?"

"Also fine."

"Good shit." Abul said, shrugging his bag onto his shoulder. "Well, as emotional as it's been, I'm afraid the time has come for me to depart this wonderful establishment and head out on a quest to find cheap booze and easy women." He raised an eyebrow as he said it, walking backwards towards the door.

"Abul, you're such a geek."

"Nerd if you please. Geek offends me."

"Sorry, nerd then."

"Oh, that reminds me. I was thinking about your mystery visitor yesterday."

"Oh?" she said, the humour wiped away in that one innocent comment.

"Yeah, I was thinking, what if it's one of your Facebook stalkers?"

"Oh, that doesn't make me feel uncomfortable at all," she said, still trying to keep the conversation light.

"No, I'm serious, who is that one guy? The one who keeps commenting on all of your photos, Billy Higglepig or something like that."

She laughed. "That's Billy Higgenbottom, and he's an old friend from school."

"But are you sure he's not a stalker?" Abul said, opening the door. "It's always the quiet ones."

"Like you?" she said, playing along.

"First off, I resent that comment. Second, I'm not a stalker. I'm a friend. Besides, I'm too much of a gigolo to get tied down with a married woman, even one as hot as you."

"Did you really just refer to yourself as a gigolo?"

"Hell yeah I did."

"I'll take that as a compliment."

"You should. It was meant as one." He said, winking. "Anyway, I better run. Places to go, people to hit on. You know the score."

"Do I?" she said, eyebrows raised.

"See you Monday Christina. Don't get too bored. Thanks again for covering for me. I owe you."

"Anytime. Good luck with the presentation, and don't get too drunk after."

"No promises, See you later." He said, leaving and letting the door close after him. She watched him go, smiling. She enjoyed the banter. There was no chemistry between them of course. It was more of a brother and sister relationship. Even so, now that he had left, the fact that she was in the store alone bothered her more than it should. Sitting on the stool by the till, she picked up her book and settled in for a long night.

#

As usual it was quiet. Between seven and midnight, she saw only a handful of customers. She was so bored she didn't even bother to profile them or make up fake histories for them. Instead, she read her book, another of those pulpy horror novels she was so fond of. People came and went, and time ticked on. A little after 11:40, she heard the distinct sound of the chime on the door as another customer came in. She gave a cursory glance towards them, seeing just a flash of a green jacket as they started to browse the shelves. Immediately losing interest, she returned to her book, hoping to finish her chapter before closing time. Her customer came to the counter, putting the double armful of goods down heavily. Christina finished the line she was reading, then looked up, gasping.

It was the woman from the white van. As if to clarify what her brain was telling her, she glanced out of the window, and sure enough, there it was. The grubby white van she had made jokes about. She considered making an apology, but couldn't think of a way to do it. Instead, she started to scan the goods and put them into bags. Napkins, paper plates, balloons.

"It's my son's birthday," the woman said, keeping a close eye on Christina.

"Oh, congratulations." She replied, hoping that if they both ignored the previous incident, it would be more comfortable all around.

"We try to do a little something for him every year. Make it special for him. This is the most special one of all."

"That's nice," Christina said, ringing the last of the items through and bagging them. "Can I get you anything else?"

"No, that's all," the woman said, still keeping those dark, inquisitive eyes locked firm.

"That will be eleven-ninety please. Any fuel?"

"Not today," the woman said, handing over a twenty.

Christina made change, handing it back to her.

"That's the thing about birthdays," the older woman said with a sigh. "So much to do no matter how far ahead you plan."

"Are you expecting many people?" Christina asked, doing the customer service thing as per the terms of her employment.

"Oh, I'm not sure yet. We only sent the invites out today." As she said it, the woman placed an invitation on the counter. For a second, Christina didn't know how to react.

Blue invite, white cake. Red lettering. She looked back at the woman who had dropped the smile and stared at Christina without anything resembling emotion.

She lurched from her seat, planning to lock herself in the staff room, and almost ran into the man, the one who had been subject of her teasing when she was with Jessie.

She drew breath just a split second before he pushed a dirty, wet rag against her face covering both her nose and mouth, wrapping his arms around her as she kicked and screamed. She flailed her arms, sending cigarettes and sweets crashing to the floor, breathing heavily and drawing in the stench of the rag. As consciousness faded, she saw the hazy ghost of the woman leaning over her and staring, those cold back eyes penetrating into the deepest reaches of her soul.

CHRISTINA

1.

Panic set in before I even had a chance to open my eyes. I had been unconscious but I hadn't forgotten what had happened: the man holding that rag to my face. Whatever was on it - whatever it was that knocked me out - I can still taste it in the back of my throat; a metallic taste making me want to retch. I opened my eyes only to see that I was no longer in the gas station. Of course I wasn't. Why would they knock me out just to leave me there? Another uncomfortable rise in my heartbeat as I realised I was tied to a bed in a dirty box room. Breeze block brickwork, bare bulb hanging from the ceiling with the light flickering, uneven concrete floor and no windows. My back was aching from the bed I was laid upon. Wooden slats with no mattress or cover, iron railings for a headboard - the part I was tied to. I sat up as best as I could but there wasn't much give in the ropes that bound me. I tried to struggle against them but the knots held fast. I went to scream out - for help - but stopped short when I saw a large note attached to the wall directly opposite the bed.

Don't scream. He doesn't like it.

Who doesn't like it? Who doesn't like me (people?) screaming? I could hear a little voice in my head telling me that - whoever it was - they didn't like people screaming because it had the potential to alert others that you were in danger. They'd hear you screaming and they'd come to help with your captors getting arrested for their efforts.

I went to scream and stopped once more.

But what if it isn't because of that? What if there is no one around who'd hear you and all you end up doing is upsetting whoever took you?

Can't risk it. If I am alone here, and I suspect I am or else they'd have been discovered already, then I need to do as they want until I can figure a way out of this.

A way out? How often in horror does the victim find their way out?

Is that what I am? The victim? My mind flashed to thoughts of my daughter; picturing her face, tears streaming down her cheeks, as she sees my photograph shown on the News channels, and in the local papers - another missing person. Another statistic. No. I won't allow it. I won't. There's a temptation to give in, wither away and fade to nothing because that's the easier path to choose but I won't. Whatever these people want, whatever their plan is - they have a fight on their hands. Just need to get myself free from these ropes.

I twisted my head and pulled my tied wrist as close to my mouth as I could get. Leaning my head the rest of the distance, I was just about able to sink my teeth into the rope's knot. To my surprise the knot wasn't as tight as it appeared and by wiggling both my wrist and tugging at the rope with my mouth, it soon came apart. With one hand freed the second rope was much easier to undo and I was soon freed.

I sat up from the bed and my aching back clicked at the lower part of my spine. It felt good but didn't take away the overall soreness.

Does your backache really matter? Get out of here!

I stood up and jumped back in fright as the door opened with no warning. A large masked man was standing there. I backed myself into the corner of the room without realising I had trapped myself. The man hesitated a moment before stepping into the room and into the little illumination offered by the flickering light.

Oh God.

A mask covered his forehead and went down to just under his mouth. His chin was visible. I had to stop myself from screaming out when I realised the mask looked like flesh stretched from one end of his face to the other; stretched so tight there were no wrinkles in it whatsoever. I instinctively raised my hands as though it would stop him from approaching me further. I could see how much my hands were shaking. He didn't move. He was just standing there, his head cocked to the side.

A deformity from where he'd continually have to crank his head to get through doorways?

He grunted. I'm not sure whether it was a word or just a sound yet I still found myself responding.

"Please don't hurt me."

He seemed to cock his head further to the side.

Does he understand me?

He stepped closer, giving me a better look at the mask; not that I wanted one. Despite being a few feet away still, I could smell it from where I was cowering. At least I presumed the smell was the mask. For all I know it could have been the man beneath it. A sweaty, rotten smell; a mix between the stink of a butchers and the rancid odour of a fish market.

"Please don't hurt me…" I repeated myself.

The closer he was now, the more the mask looked to be fake.

Please God let it be fake. A silly Halloween costume.

There was a shine to it as though it were made from latex. It can't be skin. He took another step closer and I raised my hands higher despite knowing, if he wanted to, he could easily brush them to one side with a quick swat.

Please Greg, please, come through the door - save me

from this man - a single thought rolled around in my petrified head.

What good can Greg do? He's an ant compared to this man.

I watched in horror as the man sniffed the air. For some reason, he suddenly got excited. I cried out as he rocked from side to side making a noise I can only describe as 'gorilla-like'. He took a step back away from me, still excited, and - without a proper spoken word - turned and left the room. I breathed a heavy sigh of relief despite knowing I wasn't out of the woods yet. I need to know where I am and - more specifically - I need to know how to get out of here. I waited a few seconds - still in the corner of the room - before moving to the door. I listened, my ear craned towards the doorway. I could hear the man's footsteps getting further away from me. Another sigh of relief.

Still not safe yet.

I leaned into the corridor beyond the doorway. Just a long dimly lit corridor. I can see so many doors leading off of it and more corridors between those. Where the hell am I? The temptation to call out was strong; to see if there was anyone else here in the same position as me yet I knew I couldn't. If I called out, he might come back. I made sure I walked in the opposite direction to where his footsteps had gone. I don't want to bump into him again. The next time, he might not be as happy to leave me be. I didn't run but I didn't exactly dawdle either. I'm not sure where he is or how good his hearing is. With each step I take another image of Greg and Courtney flashes through my head; even pictures of the god-awful pink and green house - who'd have thought I'd miss that in times like these?

Be home soon.

I reached the end of the corridor. There was only one way to turn and that was left. I turned and almost walked straight into a brick wall. What the hell? A dead end? I turned back around the way I came. Maybe one of the doors will lead to a way out? I don't want to run all the way to the other end of the corridor. I don't want to run in his direction. I felt my eyes well up as panic edged towards hysteria.

Keep it together, keep it together…

I nervously made my way to the first door closest to me; a closed door on my left. All the time I kept an eye out directly in front of me on the off-chance he came back into view again. Close to the door, I reached out with a still-shaking hand and gave the handle a turn. The door opened and I slipped inside without first giving the interior of the room a check; more concerned about whether *he* was coming back down my way.

Where is he? He must be close.

Inside the room I closed the door behind me. A bigger room than the one I woke up in but just as baron - more so in fact. At least the other room had the starting of a bed. In here there is only a broken chair in the middle of the room and a few pipes along the walls…

Window!

My heart skipped a beat when I noticed a window on the far wall. In my excitement I hurried over to it only to realise it was nailed shut with heavy-duty nails. Without any tools at hand, there was no way I was going to get out of it and it's not big enough to crawl through if I were to smash the glass. Damn! Damn! Damn! I looked beyond the grimy glass into the world beyond, the freedom so tantalisingly close, and felt my eyes well up once more.

Hold it together. It's not over yet. There must be a way out of here.

Beyond the initial dirt track which I presumed surrounded the building, there was a lush meadow of green leading onto what looked to be a thick forest. Both a nice sight and also a curse as it meant we were in the middle of nowhere - so chances of rescue were slim - but at least, if I found a way out, it would be easy to hide from my captors by heading into the forests. A loud cry from further down the corridor pulled my attention back to the fact I needed to get out of here before dreaming of hiding amongst the woodlands. Another cry; one of frustration? I temporarily froze on the spot by the window; a little sun-light spilling in through the narrow window, warming my face and reminding me that there was everything to fight for. Beyond that window lies freedom, my family, and my life. I want it back. Another cry. It sounded angrier this time. My damned heart was beating so hard it felt as though it were going to explode. I took a deep breath, in an effort to slow the beating, and hurried into the corner of the room, behind the open door. The way he keeps crying out, I'm sure it is because he's realised I've left the room he'd seen me in. It won't be long before he starts looking for me. All I can hope is he doesn't search each room thoroughly before going off down another corridor, perhaps even leading me to my safety without realising?

A shimmer of hope.

A shimmer of hope unless he finds me here first, that is.

From the corridor, I heard him scream out with fear before hearing his quickened footsteps getting more distant from where I was. Relief washed through me, albeit short-lived relief. Voices beyond the door, closer than his footsteps had been. Another sound too - getting closer. Is something being dragged?

I jumped when the door suddenly opened a little wider, nearly hitting me directly in the face as I backed myself up against the wall, trying to make myself as flat as I possibly could. Voices.

"Over there," a woman said.

I recognised the voice. Was she the woman who'd spoken to me at the gas station? She was! I know she was. I held my breath in an effort to be as quiet as possible as I listened to what they were doing.

"A little help wouldn't go amiss," came a man's voice.

A heavy dragging sound as they moved across the room; thankfully to the left of where I was standing so I was still invisible to them.

"Well if you hadn't startled him, perhaps he would have helped."

"Had I not startled him, he would have seen his present."

The dragging noise stopped.

"Here," said the woman. She handed something metal over to the man, clinking it together in the process giving away its material. "That pipe should be strong enough."

I heard a pipe moving slightly from side to side; a loud clanking noise.

"It's not going anywhere," the man said.

A metal sounding 'click', followed by metal hitting metal and another metallic 'click'.

"Okay?" the woman asked.

Another sound of a pipe clanking from side to side as it was tested for strength.

"Yes."

"Come on then. Did you want to give him his other present now?" the woman asked.

The voices muffled as they walked from the room, closing the door behind them revealing what the dragging noise had been. A man - similar to my own age

- was cuffed to the pipe. Just as I had been, he was out cold. I hurried over to his side and knelt down on the hard floor beside him. I noticed for the first time there was a small cube shaped parcel next to his body.

Ignore it, it's not important.

"Hello?" I shook him from side to side, trying to wake him up. The way I saw it - two heads were better than one and we'd be able to help each other get out of here. "Can you hear me?" he wasn't stirring. I took a hold of his wrist and paused, waiting to feel for a pulse.

There it is.

"Can you hear me? You have to wake up!" I shook him harder.

"I don't think he is going to wake up," I startled at the sound of a female voice behind me. I jumped up and spun around. The old woman was standing there, her arms folded across her chest and a disappointed look on her face. The old man who'd taken me by surprise at the gas station was behind her.

There's no way out.

"Please, what do you want with me?" I asked.

"Well for starters - you could pass me my son's present," she said. She pointed to the box on the floor next to the unconscious stranger. Nervously, keeping one eye on the couple, I picked it up off the floor and tossed it towards the woman. She caught it and thanked me.

"I want to go home."

"You can," the old woman said, "after my son's birthday party. You're guest of honour."

"What are you talking about?"

"You did get the invitation, didn't you?" she asked.

"I just want to go home now." I paused a moment before trying to appeal to their humanity, "I'm scared."

"You should be, he can be quite unpredictable, but - between you and I - I think he is going to like you."

The old man whispered to what must have been his wife, "You said that last time."

Why did the old woman shrug?

"Please, I have a daughter. I need to go home."

"Would you do anything for your daughter?" the old woman asked me. I nodded. "That's good. Any parent should do whatever they can for their children. It's the way it should be. You'd do anything for your daughter, I'd do anything for my son..."

"She'll be scared if I don't go home."

"I told you - you will go home - just as soon as the party is over."

"What party?!" I shouted.

Someone screamed from somewhere down the corridor. It was him.

"Please don't shout. He doesn't like it when people shout."

"Just let me go home."

"You're starting to sound like a broken record," the old lady pointed out.

I screamed at her, "JUST LET ME GO HOME!"

Another scream from down the corridor.

I kept repeating the sentence as loudly as I could, again and again - each time my scream was echoed by a scream from him, wherever he was. The old man suddenly lunged towards me with his hands raised; one around my throat and the other over my mouth. I fell back against the wall where he pinned me.

"You need to shut your fucking mouth," he hissed, "because you're upsetting the boy. You keep upsetting him and we can't be held accountable for his actions, okay?" I didn't move. He pulled me away from the wall for a moment before slamming back against it, "I said okay?" I nodded. "Now, you're going to come back to your room, and you're going to let us put you back on the bed until he is ready to get to know you!"

Tears down my cheeks.

The old man continued, "And if you do what we say, how we say it - you can go home after his party. How does that sound? Do you want that?" I nodded again. "Good." With no more words, and keeping control of me with his hand clamped around my throat in a vice-like grip, the man pulled me from where he'd pinned me to the wall and shoved me out into the corridor, facing the way I'd originally come from. The old woman closed the door behind us as she followed.

At the far end of the corridor I could see the man lurking within the shadows watching us with a curious fascination. I tried not to look at him. I closed my eyes and relied on the old man to guide me back to the room. It wasn't long before we turned to the right and I opened my eyes again. There was the bed I'd earlier woken on.

2.

"Lie down," the old man hissed. I didn't argue with
him. I just laid there as he started to tie me back to the
headboard. I had so many questions racing through my
mind and yet didn't dare ask any one of them. "Now, he
might take a little time to warm to you but that doesn't
give you the right to treat him badly, okay?" He finished
tying me and looked me in the face, "Okay?" I nodded.
"Good girl." He moved away from the bed and went to
stand in the doorway.

The old woman walked in and placed the cube-shaped
parcel next to me on the bed, "Be sure that he gets this
won't you, dear?" She didn't wait for an answer. She
walked from the room, followed by the old man. With
the door left open I watched as they turned right and
disappeared down the corridor; their footsteps getting
fainter.

I immediately turned my head to either side, looking
at the knots around my wrists. They were much, much
tighter this time.

Still possible.

Satisfied the old couple was distant enough from me
that they wouldn't hear me moving around on the bed I
followed the same tactic that saw me released the first
time I found myself in this position. Wrist stretched to
me and head leaning right over in order to nibble at the
ropes. I went to start with the left hand wrist and froze
immediately; something standing in my peripheral
vision.

Him.

I twisted my head to the doorway. He was standing
there, watching me. His head cranked to the side again. I

swallowed hard in an effort to clear my voice for when I spoke. I wanted to sound as calm as possible; let him know that I'm not scared of him nor am I worried about where I am.

"Hello," I said.

He stepped to the side, disappearing back into the corridor. I knew he was still standing there. I could hear him breathing; a heavy wheezing of a severe asthmatic. I fidgeted on the bed to see if I could catch eye contact with him but I couldn't get the angle. I needed him to know I wasn't a threat. I needed him to know I welcomed him here. Whatever he wanted, if I don't fight, if I just let it happen then it will be easier. It might not be what I want but I have to remember my daughter. I don't want her growing up without a mother. I'll do anything to get back home to her.

"I know you're there," I continued. I paused hoping he'd come back into the room so that I could talk to him, maybe even convince him into letting me go. "Don't you want to come and talk to me?" In my head I kept hearing the old woman's advice; *he doesn't like screaming.* I kept my voice low on purpose. I don't want to make him angry.

He'd crush me.

"What's your name?" I asked. I thought he could - at the very least - talk to me from where he was hiding himself. Slowly he leaned his head around the corner of the doorway. He stared right at me and grunted something I couldn't quite understand. Did he speak or just make a noise? "My name is Christina, it's a pleasure to meet you." Despite my best efforts, I could hear the shaking in my voice. I only hoped he couldn't. Without a word he charged into the room and grabbed the parcel that lay next to me on the bed. I betrayed my attempt to remain calm by jumping and letting out a little squeal.

He just froze, parcel in hand, and looked at me - head
cocked right over to one side. "I'm sorry," I said, "you
startled me." He hissed at me and disappeared beyond
the doorway once more. Again, I knew he was standing
there. I could hear him playing with the parcel; shaking
it from side to side as though unsure of what to make of
it.

"It's a present," I called out.

He stopped moving. The wheezy breathing gave him
away though; he was still there.

"It's from your mum and dad," I told him. "Is it your
birthday?" I asked. Both the old woman and the old man
had suggested it was but - given the situation - I wasn't
sure whether what they were saying was true or not. "If
you untie me, I can help you open it."

He grunted.

Don't push to be untied. Show him you're relaxed.

There was silence before he re-appeared in the
doorway, the parcel still clutched in his large hand. I
smiled at him despite yearning to scream.

"Do you know what it is?" I asked him.

He looked down at the parcel - wrapped in a brown
paper - and looked back up to me and grunted. He shook
the box once more causing something to rattle within.

"Be careful!" I told him. "It might be fragile." He
cocked his head back to the other side as he looked at
me. His dark eyes, visible behind the mask, had an air of
confusion about them. If this was his birthday, was it the
first one he'd ever experienced? It's hard to pin an age
on him, given the mask, but his height and sheer bulk
suggested he wasn't a teenager. Possibly my own age?

All the missing people have been around my age.
Don't think about that now.

"Why don't you open it?" I urged him. All the time he
had something else to focus open, he wasn't focusing

upon me. He looked at me. Beyond the mask, the same look of confusion I'd seen a minute ago. "They said it was your birthday. Do you know what that means?" I asked him. He hissed again, making me jump. I composed myself, "Your mum and dad said you were having a party. Do you like the sound of a party?" He looked at me.

"P-a-r-t-y?!" he wheezed. I was shocked to hear him speak. I thought he couldn't. I was still unsure as to whether he was able to understand the words I was saying, or even the word he'd just spoken though. I nodded back towards the parcel, "That's your birthday present. You normally get them at your party but your mum let you have it now. That was nice of her, wasn't it?"

He hissed again and bounded from the room. The door slammed shut.

What did I say?

I listened as he bounded down the corridor once more. Another door slammed shut.

Alone again.

The temptation was to start gnawing at the restraints once more but I was nervous of either the parents or the son coming back again. What if I break free again and the next time they don't just put me back here? The old man has it in him to hurt me, I felt it when he put his hand around my throat and squeezed. I could tell it won't take much to anger him. Any of them, come to that. They're all just as unstable as the other. I waited there, in the dimly lit room, unsure of what my next move should be; my mind turning back to thoughts of my daughter. By now, they must know I'm missing. Someone from the station must have told them, perhaps calling my home to see why I wasn't at work? It dawned on me that I wouldn't need to do anything. I have a family, I had responsibilities in the station; people would have known fast that something was wrong. People would have known I was missing and alerted the proper authorities.

But was the Closed Circuit Television working?

I felt a horrible sinking sensation. I had been telling my managers for a while now that the CCTV wasn't recording as it should have been. Some days it worked, some days it didn't. Somehow it had developed one of those irritating intermittent faults; one day it will be okay, the next it will just pack up - sometimes deleting what was already stored on the hard-drive. It had been an ongoing issue for over a month and it wasn't just me who reported it; other staff members had mentioned it too. I know I only work thirty hours a week and there are plenty of times it could have been dealt with but no one has ever mentioned it. I guess, thinking about it as only I can, there is no reason to say it has been done. I'm not a manager after all. What does it matter if I don't know it's been fixed or not?

Please God let it have been fixed.

If it was working then most of the store will be covered with the four internal cameras. There are a couple of external cameras too meaning the forecourt is covered as well. If the cameras are working, so long as the recording stations haven't been destroyed, then everything that happened to me would have been caught on tape. They'd have me serving the customers, they'd have my colleague going home for the night and they'd have the old couple. The cameras outside will have the vehicle and the registration plates.

Please God let it have been fixed.

#

I woke with a start. He was standing at the end of the bed, grunting like an excited animal. He was holding something up for me to see. I had to concentrate on focusing my eyes. My vision was foggy I was so tired. He was holding what appeared to be a Jack-in-the-box toy; a tatty box, dirtied through age with a silver crank sticking from the side. Going by the shape, I guessed he'd figured out how to open his parcel.

"From your mum and dad?" I asked.

He grunted and rocked from side to side.

"Do you know how to use it?" Despite being tied at the wrists still, I motioned for him to come closer to me. He hesitated but took a step forward.

Oh good. Progress. Just what you wanted.

"If you untie me, I'll show you." I said, pushing my luck.

He took a step back and growled. Although scared for my life and missing my family, I couldn't help but feel sorry for him. I wasn't sure what was wrong with him, I wasn't sure what his story was, but clearly he had issues and - despite what I feared - so far he seemed more scared of me than I was of him - and that's saying something.

I turned the conversation back to the box in the hope of winning his trust again, "You see that bit sticking from the side of it?" I nodded towards the box. He looked down to it. "If you turn that, and keep turning it, something will pop out."

He shook the box.

Idiot.

"No - turn the handle."

He looked at me and grunted.

I tried spelling it out slowly for him, "H A N D L E."

"Handle," he repeated in his wheezy voice.

"Yes," I said. I nodded to give him further encouragement. "Turn it."

He grunted and shook the box again. I went to tell him what to do again but realised he'd frozen perfectly still, his eyes - still behind that mask - now fixed from me to the door. He sniffed the air and hissed.

"What's wrong?" I asked.

"Good morning!" the old woman's voice made me jump and the man hiss again. "Oh do stop that, child," she berated him. He immediately retreated to the corner of the room, huddling into the corner. I noticed she had a tray in her hands; scrambled eggs on toast on a paper plate, plastic cutlery to the side of it along with a small sachet of tomato sauce and a packet of black pepper. "I came to see you last night," she was talking to me now, "but you were sound asleep."

"You said I was guest of honour at his party and then I could go home... When is his party?"

"Soon - of course - we just have to finish a few preparations. You'll be pleased to hear it's look lovely though and we have a full turn out of guests."

"There're guests already here? Then you don't need me. Please let me go home to my daughter. She'll be scared."

"If you want we can invite her too?"

"No!"

A scream from the corner of the room.

"Well then, be quiet. You're his special guest anyway. We have plans for you, young lady." She sat on what passed as a bed, next to where I laid. She put the tray on her lap and started forking some egg onto it before passing it across to just in front of my mouth. "Eat up," she ordered me. "You need to keep your strength up."

"For what?"

She sighed, clearly getting impatient with me, "For the party." I didn't open my mouth. For all I know it could be laced with all sorts of crap. I won't eat it. I would rather starve to death. "Not eating?" I shook my head. "Suit yourself. You can have it at lunchtime."

"I won't eat it."

"Then for dinner."

"You're not listening to me."

"Then you can go hungry. We don't waste food here."

"Why don't you let him have it?" he was watching us, his eyes seemingly fixed upon the plate.

"Silly girl, he doesn't eat this. He's a growing lad…" she laughed and went to leave the room. She stopped in the doorway and looked towards her son. She noticed the box in his hands, "Do you like your gift?" she asked.

He grunted. I'm not sure whether it was because he understood her or because he was reacting to the kindness in her tone.

Kindness?

"If you turn the handle, it plays music!" she said. "You know you like your music."

"Music!" he wheeze, he shook the box.

The old lady smiled at him, "He'll get it soon enough I'm sure," and walked from the room leaving the two of us together again.

"Music!" he repeated, standing to his full height - holding the box out in front of him. "Music!"

"Turn the handle," I told him, forcing myself to swallow back the tears that desperately wanted to shed. My voice cracked and I couldn't help but start to cry, "Just turn the fucking handle," I kept telling him over and over despite the fact he didn't understand at me. I felt my fear and frustration continue to grow until I couldn't help but to scream out at the top of my lungs. He immediately screamed back with his face close to mine. Eye to eye I can see an anger bubbling away close to the surface. "I'm sorry, I'm sorry, I'm sorry…" I kept whispering.

A scream came from down the corridor.

The man they dragged in must be awake.

I didn't dare respond to the captive man's cries, not whilst this man was so close to my face; his stinking breath filling my nostrils.

Please don't hurt me.

He cranked his head to a near upright position and stood to his full height. I felt my blood pressure rise and my heart beat faster as he loomed over me, his toy box firmly gripped in his hand as though he wanted to bash my head in with it.

"I have a daughter," I told him, my voice shaking as I struggled to control my emotions. "I'm a mummy," I said. I hoped he understood what it was to be a mother. I hoped he thought about his own mum and likened me to her. He stopped staring at me and looked back down to the box in his hands before taking a large step back. I breathed a sigh of relief.

"Can you hear me?" the man from the other room shouted. I could. I wondered if the son heard him too? He was looking down at his box, still visibly trying to figure it out. I prayed the man in the other room would shut up for his own safety. The tall man before me lifted his head once more, as though alert. He sniffed the air, turned around and left the room - slamming the door behind him. I immediately started gnawing at the ropes once more. I can't stay here, I can't just rely on the fact they said they were going to let me go. I can't count on the CCTV at work being fixed either. It would be stupid to do so. The old couple said I could go home after the party but of course they aren't going to release me. They can't risk me going straight to the cops - and I would to save anyone else having to suffer this. The longer I stay here, like this, the more likely it is that I will die here. I stopped suddenly at the musical sound of *Ring-a-ring-a-roses*. I guess he managed to get into the box finally. The music stopped and he screamed. I couldn't help but scream out too, scared of his reaction to his present and the mood it might put him in.

Please God, help me!

I wept.

"Hello?!" the other prisoner (I presume) called out from down the corridor.

Please be quiet, you're only going to attract unwanted attention.

At the moment he was safer than me, the old woman's son didn't know he was there. At least I don't think he knew he was there. That man - whoever he was - was in a much better position than I was. For a couple of minutes he did go quiet, making me think he'd sensed my wishes for him to do so. The silence was short-lived as he let out a scream. A scream echoed by the son.

3.

Despite previous intentions to keep pulling at the ropes until they gave, I found myself lying there - listening to the sounds of the building. The occasional creak from floorboards upstairs - telling me that the old couple were milling around above us, or there were even more people here - and the other prisoner down the corridor. Despite the door being shut I could occasionally still hear him calling out for someone. I wanted to shout out to him, let him know I was here. I wanted him to know he wasn't alone. Common sense suggested I kept myself to myself. If I get out of here, I'll go and find him. Until then, I need to remain quiet.

Can't upset the son.

The door opened and startled me. I was so busy concentrating on the sounds at the far end of the building that I hadn't paid attention to what was beyond my own door.

"I thought you might be hungry," the old woman was standing there with the tray of food she'd earlier tried to pass off as breakfast. She smiled, "Can you hear them?" she nodded down the corridor, towards the room she'd dumped the man in, along with her husband. "It's so sweet."

I listened.

"Hello? Who's there?" I heard the man ask, his voice muffled slightly by the distance between us.

"Hello? Who's there?" the wheezing, deep voice of the son responded.

"Look - I think there's been a misunderstanding…"

"Look," the son repeated, "I think there's been a misunderstanding."

"Why are you doing this?"

"Why are you doing this?"

"Please - stop it!" I heard the man beg.

"Please - stop it!"

The pair fell silent. The old woman turned to me, "It's nice to hear him talk. He doesn't really say much anymore."

"Who are you people?" I asked.

"Did Jim put you up to this?" the captive man asked, breaking the silence between the two of them.

"Did Jim put you up this this?" The son repeated the question back to him again.

"Then who?"

"Then who?"

"WHO THE FUCK ARE YOU?!" The sudden raised voice made me jump. The old woman just stood there and closed her eyes. She sighed heavily.

"That was brief then," she said - a disappointed tone in her voice.

The son screamed out again, startling me once more.

"You get used to it," the old woman said. She stepped into the room and pulled the door shut, trapping us both in there. "He'll be okay," she said. I wasn't sure who she was referring to; her son or the man cuffed to the pipework. Beyond the closed door I could hear footsteps pounding their way down the corridor; heavy thumps getting nearer and nearer. I breathed a sigh of relief as they went straight by the door to my room.

My room?

I jumped again as another door shut. I went to say something but the old woman shushed me quiet before I had the chance. A second later and classical music started playing loudly.

She smiled, "He always plays this when he is upset."

"Who was that?" I asked. "Who upset him? Another guest?"

"Another guest? Oh God no, we have quite enough of those."

"Then who is it?" I demanded to know. If I was going to be here, captive, then I needed to know what was going on. I deserved that much.

"Don't raise your voice with me, young lady. He might like you but believe me, I am quite indifferent to you." She set the tray down on the floor, next to the bed, and turned back to the door. She held her hand out and twisted the handle.

"Wait," I said. "Please. I need to use the toilet."

She hesitated and pulled the door shut again. She slowly turned to face me, "Now listen carefully, if you try anything… If you ruin this party… You're never going to get out of here. We will also be forced to bring someone else in to be guest of honour. Someone, say, like your daughter. Do you understand me?"

I nodded.

"Good." She reached under the bed and pulled out a silver, dented bucket. She placed it in the corner of the room and came back to the bed. With steady hands, she started undoing the ropes around my wrists.

First one clear.

My wrists felt so sore. I slowly brought my hand down to my side, stretching out the fingers as I did so. So much more comfortable. I wonder whether she'll allow me to be tied to the sides of the bed, if she forces me to be tied up again that is.

Second wrist clear.

I did the same again with my second hand; pins and needles tingling both hands.

"Be quick," the old lady said, nodding towards the bucket.

96

"You want me to go in there?" I asked. I didn't know what I expected differently.

"Unless you don't really need to go?"

"I do." I walked over to the bucket and went to undo my jeans. The old lady was just standing there, watching me. "Could you at least turn around?" I asked. She folded her arms and raised an eyebrow. I sighed and undid my jeans, pulling them down to round my ankles, along with my underwear. I squatted over the bucket. Despite the need to go, I couldn't. Not with her watching me. She tilted her head to the side as she stared between my legs, a smile on her face.

"Tidy," she said. "He's going to be very impressed."

Her words sent a cold shudder down my spine. I shuffled my way around the bucket so she only had a side-view of me. Feeling degraded, I felt my face redden as my pee slowly started to trickle noisily into the bucket.

"I don't suppose you have any tissue?" I asked as I finished my business. She didn't move. "I didn't think so." I pulled my jeans and underwear up; a little part of me wishing the ground would just open up and swallow me down. "What should I do with the bucket?" I asked.

"I'm sure you'll need it again at some point, just leave it there."

We were standing opposite each other. She still had her arms folded over one another in front of her whereas mine were hanging freely by my side. I knew she was expecting me to get back onto the bed but I didn't want to. The door had a lock on it; couldn't she just lock me in here? It's not as though I can get out.

"Back on the bed," the old lady said, dashing my hopes of being left to roam the room.

"The man - the one who is having the party - who is he to you? Is he really your son?" I asked in a hope of buying myself a little more time without being tied down.

"You know he is. I told you."

"What's wrong with him?" I asked.

The old lady's back stiffened as she stood up straight. "What's wrong with you?" she hissed.

"No, I didn't mean… I'm sorry. I didn't mean to offend you."

Well done.

"Get back on the bed and be thankful my husband wasn't in here to hear that."

"He just seems very nervous around people," I said, trying to make it sound less bad than it had come across.

"Get back on the bed!" the old lady hissed again.

Reluctantly I walked the few steps across the room to the bed and made myself as comfortable as possible on it; knowing there wasn't a mattress that wasn't easy. The old lady grabbed at my wrists and yanked my hands above my head once more. I didn't bother asking her to tie them by my side - to one of the wooden slats. Given her mood, I knew the answer. Besides which, from that position I wouldn't be able to try and bite my way through the restraints - something I intend to do the moment I am given some peace and quiet. I lay perfectly still - and quiet as a mouse - as the old lady started to tie my wrists to the headboard once more. She was muttering something under her breath. I couldn't make it all out but it was something to do with her son. Something like 'of course he's nervous, he's always down here'. She finished what she was doing and stood up straight, giving the ropes a final tug to ensure they were tight enough (they were).

"I'm sorry," I told her, "I didn't mean to offend you."

I don't care. I'm playing nice.

"I didn't think." I continued. The old lady didn't say anything. She simply stared at me for a moment and then left the room after opening the door, leaving the tray on the floor.

"Hello?!" the man was calling from down the corridor. The old lady shook her head and slammed the door shut leaving me to my own stupid thoughts.

You've done it now, you stupid woman.

My eyes started to well up again as thoughts of my daughter crept into my head. I was sure I wouldn't see her again, or Greg. My brain was desperately trying to cast itself back to the last time I told them that I loved them. I couldn't remember. Why couldn't I remember? All I seem to recall were the sarcastic comments I'd made to them after they'd say something particularly stupid. Why did I always have to be so sarcastic? Why couldn't I have been more vocal with my true feelings? I'd give anything to have one more conversation with them. Just five minutes on the phone - or something - so I could tell them both how much I loved them. Five minutes to tell them not to worry about me; I'm not scared where I am.

A lie.

Maybe if I promise to be well behaved at the party and not embarrass anyone, the old couple might let me use the phone. I know they keep saying they're going to let me go as soon as the party is done but I know they won't. I know they're just going to kill me.

Crying now.

I closed my eyes and tried to take myself to a better place; a kinder place. Lush green fields with a blanket set in the middle of it. A picnic with a forest in the background of the picturesque settings, perfect blue skies, and a hot sun beating down upon us; Greg, Courtney and myself. Laughter at jokes and stories we share. No arguments, no tears, no stress - just a chilled atmosphere; a memory from two summers ago.

When you open your eyes you will be back there. Transported.

Is that possible? When I open my eyes - will I have somehow transported back to the happier, safer time playing in my memory? Please let it be possible… Sausage rolls, juice boxes, some fruit, sandwiches… Sandwiches? What flavours?

Anything but Peanut Butter….

My mouth started to water as I pictured all of the foods I'd like at my picnic. Each time a new image popped into my head my mouth watered that little bit more as I imagined the taste. I pictured having my Kindle device with me too - loaded with new horror books I'd be longing to read from my favourite authors; Stephen King and Dean Koontz to name but two. Unable to take it any longer, and with my fingers crossed, I opened my eyes in the hope of being transported to where I'd imagined. My heart sunk. Of course I hadn't gone anywhere. Here I am, on the bed. Trapped.

Please God, take me away from all of this.

God isn't listening.

God is dead.

More damned tears. Try it again. Close your eyes. Imagine you're at that picnic. When you open them again, you'll be back there but you need to really try hard.

I closed my eyes. I imagined walking barefoot through the long grass, each blade tickling the underside of my foot. I pictured the birds nesting in the trees, some of them soaring through the skies so blue, singing without a care in the world. Courtney and Greg were laughing about something; their laughter carrying across the otherwise peaceful meadows. I imagined myself turning to see them. I'd be smiling that they were having fun together. I'd wave at them - first Greg would wave, as he often kept one eye on me, and then my daughter would wave. I'd imagine walking back over to them, after they called me to do so. I'd be smiling broadly, and Greg would give me a wink.

Good. Now open your eyes.

I opened my eyes and jumped. The old man was standing before me with a rag in his hands. He lunged forward and held it to my face. I struggled against the ropes but... Dizzy... Foggy head... Eyelids heavy. Blurred vision.... Struggle to focus... The old lady walked past the doorway with an axe.. Body relaxed... Eyes shut. Complete blackness. Sounds fade.

SHAW / BRAY

INTERVAL

SHAW / BRAY

R Y A N

1.

My head was lifted from where I laid. Felt groggy. A good thing someone was helping to lift it. Someone? "Who's there?" I slurred. Still drunk? Eyes won't open. The fuck? "Hello?" Did I say hello or did it come out as mumbled as I heard it? Was that even a word? I opened my mouth. No I didn't. I didn't do that. Someone opened my mouth. Tried to speak again but the word - whatever it was going to be - came out more like an 'aaaah' noise. A sweet taste in my mouth. What is that? Is that my saliva? Tastes good. Ssh. Someone's there. Don't say a word and especially don't roar. You are not a dinosaur.

#

Ryan was lying on a comfortable looking bed, despite the sheets being heavily stained with blood. His blood. The old man was sitting on the edge of the bed next to him, a needle-less syringe in his hand - now empty from where the content had been squirted into Ryan's mouth; liquid morphine. The old man carefully put Ryan's head back down on the pillow and set the syringe to one side just as the old lady - his wife - came back in.

"What are you doing? Was that your morphine?" she asked.

He nodded, "I don't need it; I feel fine."

"But you're not fine." The old lady looked at Ryan. He looked a mess and not just because she'd cut his arm off with a fire-axe after losing the keys to the handcuffs.

The wound was stitched up by the old lady before he lost so much blood that he died; a perk of being a nurse many moons ago. His skin was pale and sweaty and his eyes were rolling around in the back of his head. "How much have you given him?"

"Enough to keep him quiet, not enough to kill him."

"And how much have you got left for yourself?" she asked.

"Does it matter?"

"You're a fool. You're wasting your medicine on someone who isn't going to survive the night anyway. You know you're going to need it."

"I'm dead anyway, just as he is. I haven't lost an arm, I can suffer in silence. I doubt very much that he'll be able to. Do you want him crying out during the party and scaring the boy? Especially today of all days, when we need him to stay calm and controllable." He stood up and walked from the room.

The old lady followed him, "Where are you going? You should be resting!"

"I'm going to check everything is set up as it should be. It will be time enough to start the proceedings soon enough," the old man snapped back, irritated that his wife had dared question his actions. There was a time when she wouldn't question anything. What he said - went. That was it. It wouldn't have been up for discussion, and they certainly wouldn't have argued about it. But since the illness took a hold - damned cancer - his wife was trying to take charge more and more and he hated it. They walked down a narrow corridor into a large room. The whole side wall was a giant window - covered up with sheets of wood; some parts taped. In the middle of the room was a grand table with chairs lining either side; one chair at the head. The table was so big it had taken a couple of large, white sheets to cover it. In front of each chair was a place-setting with a paper plate, a napkin on top of it.

"When are the guests getting here?" the old man snapped to his wife.

"When we're ready." She changed the subject, "So what do you think of the room?" She had set the room up whilst he had been napping (which was most of the time); the table in the middle, the walls on either side had 'birthday boy' banners stretched across them in various places and at different angles, and a smaller table had been set up underneath the covered window which had been loaded with buffet food: cocktail sausages, chocolate fingers, quiches, cheese on sticks, your typical party food. "All I need to do is finish off the cake, bring in the guests - not forgetting the guest of honour, who I still need to dress - and then it will be ready for our boy," she smiled.

"Good." He rubbed his side as though in discomfort.

"Are you okay?" she asked, a genuine look of concern on her face.

"Let's just get this done." He laughed, forgetting his pain for a moment, "I'm looking forward to seeing his face. Boy's in for a treat! Oh to be twenty years younger…"

The old lady gave him a playful slap on the arm, "Behave yourself." Knowing he was joking, she changed the subject, "I'm going to get working. Take a seat, I'll shout if I need you."

He nodded, "A good idea." She watched as he stumbled his way from the room, his hand clutched to his side which was obviously hurting him. She knew he was getting weaker. She knew time was against them. She just hoped he'd live long enough to see everything through to the end. Despite her hope, she knew it was a tall order.

\#

When the old lady moves she leaves ghost-like images of herself; like a hundred million shadows cast. I don't know how she does it but it looks amazing and I can't help but giggle every time she does something. I want to lift my head up to have a look around but it feels like a deadweight. Annoying me really because I want to know what she's doing; pulling out all of the chairs from around my bed. And speaking of my bed - what was wrong with the last one? It was comfortable at least. This one is weird. It's shaped like a table. Even had novelty place settings around me. When Jema and I have this baby, I won't buy him a table shaped bed. It's boring. I'll buy him one shaped like a racing car like what I wanted when I was growing up. I should totally go and buy myself one of those tomorrow. Jema can steer it whilst I tailgate her arse. Am I laughing? I feel like I should be laughing. Oh, hello, the old lady is looking at me. She's pretty. I'll give her one of my special smiles. She said something - I'm not sure what, it sounded echoey - and walked from the room. I could hear her next door, banging around making all kinds of noise. I tried to get up to see what she was doing but nothing seems to be working as it should. Panic over; the lady came back in wheeling someone in a wheelchair. I said hello. I think I said hello. No, I definitely said hello. She helped the man from the wheelchair to one of the empty seats around my bed. Is he saying hello back to me? I can't tell. With him in the chair, staring at me, the lady disappeared from the room again. Further banging and crashing around next door and she came back; the wheelchair pushed in front of her with another person.

"Hello," I definitely said that.

"Be quiet," the lady hissed at me.

"You're rude," I told her. "Who are your friends?"

"They're not my friends," she said. Among the blurred images she was creating of herself, I could tell she was helping this person into another of the empty chairs too.

"That's rude," I pointed out to her once more, "they can hear you. Apologise."

So many blurred images; is she shaking her head at me?

"Your friends aren't saying much," I pointed out. "It's not going to be the liveliest of parties, is it? Especially as your boy isn't very chatty either. It's a room full of retards," I started to laugh.

"Of course they're not very talkative. They're dead."

I was really laughing now, "You're weird."

#

Ryan was lying in the middle of the grand table in what was set up as the party room. He was completely naked with his head lolling from side to side from where he was unable to control his muscles properly. The old lady was busy wheeling in rotten corpses from one of the rooms adjacent to this one; each time setting them up at the table around Ryan.

The dead bodies were previous guests to the large three story building they'd turned into their home; an old abandoned warehouse out in the middle of nowhere that they'd taken for themselves. The guests weren't meant to have ended up dead; that was never the intention when bringing them. It's just - their son never found anyone he'd truly gotten on with. The people would scare him, often just by screaming for their freedom, and he'd react violently. He was a big man; one violent outburst was often all it took to silence his supposed-friends for the rest of their lives.

The whole downstairs of the warehouse had been sectioned off, with exits bricked shut. There was a narrow opening which could squeeze a body through (a necessity), crafted by the head of the family to make their lives easier when moving people in and out, but that was locked via a heavy-duty padlock. From the upstairs, the only way down was via a secret passage the father dug out for them with a false wall at the end of it. The only way up to the second floor from the outside of the building - where the 'main house' was built - was via a ladder from the outside of the building; a fire ladder which climbed to the top of the building. You'd climb up it and then clamber across to one of the smashed windows which, coincidentally, was one of the only windows on the second storey not to be boarded up.

Downstairs had taken several years - most of their son's childhood - to construct and now it was nothing but a series of shoddily built corridors and near empty rooms; as much a prison for him as it was for any friends his dad had sent his way. Truth be told - had a person had a brain cell, or not been restrained down there - it wouldn't have been too hard for them to find a way out. The mother was a little worried about this, at first, but soon had her worries quashed when the first corpse came to light. She'd taken the guest some food down and panicked for a moment when she realised he wasn't where she'd left him. Setting the tray to one side, she quickly scoured the area only to find the mangled body elsewhere with her son sitting next to it, eating at the flesh as though it were a perfect cut of pork. They'd hoped his eating habits were to be a one off - a weird form of experimentation on his part - but that wasn't to

be the case. The more people died, the more they had a
bite taken from them.

And that was where Ryan came in.

2.

The old lady entered the room, pushing a trolley in front of her. She wheeled it up to the table, now completely surrounded by corpses in various degrees of decomposition and stopped it next to where Ryan laid. Only four chairs remained empty. The one at the head of the table, one on the left, and two on the right: reserved seats for the guest of honour, their son, and - of course - the mother and father.

"I feel funny," he complained. His eyes were still rolling around in his skull and it was obvious he was having problems focusing.

"You can blame my husband for that," the old lady moaned.

"Who? The old man? That's your husband? I thought he was your dad!" Ryan's speech was heavy and slurred as he struggled through his near-overdose. He noticed the trolley, "What's that for?" he asked.

"I'm going to make my son a cake," the old lady said.

"That's nice," he slurred. "I think I scared your son," he confessed. "I yelled at him because he was just looking at me."

"Why would you do that?" the lady asked as she picked up a scalpel from the trolley.

"I didn't realise he was simple."

"I'd rather you didn't talk about him like that," she said, her tone was strict.

"I'm going to be a father," Ryan said. "Jema - that's my girlfriend - she is expecting our first baby."

"That's nice."

"I think it's great you're doing this for your son, he's lucky to have you." Ryan tried to lift his head from the table once more to address the dead bodies sitting around him, "And he's lucky to have such good friends as yourselves," he continued, still blissfully unaware in his drugged up state that the people around him were deceased. "Is there going to be a cake?" Ryan turned his attention back to the lady with the scalpel. "You need cake at a birthday party, don't you?"

"You do and - yes - there will be a cake."

She leaned over Ryan's body and made a small slit in his chest with the razor-sharp blade.

"Hey!" he moaned.

"Try and lie still."

"What are you doing?"

"I'm making a series of small incisions. Nothing to worry about," she said as she cut him again. A small cut about a centimetre in length.

"Oh okay. It feels funny," he said.

She cut him again.

"Is this a party game, or something?" he slurred, his head rolled to the side.

"You'll see," she said.

Another cut.

"I like party games. Will I be able to have a go?"

"Maybe."

Another cut.

"I was always good at pin the tail on the donkey," he said.

Another cut.

"But I never managed to win at pass the parcel. I don't like pass the parcel."

"Uh huh."

Another cut.

"And don't even get me started on musical chairs. Once, when I was younger, I was playing it and someone

pulled a chair for me when I was about to sit down. I fell
on the floor. It hurt," he laughed.

"Try not to move."

Another cut.

The blood was trickling from each of the wounds on
his chest, running down the sides of his chest and onto
the white table cloth, staining it red.

"I'm sorry," he slurred.

"That's okay."

Another cut.

"What's your son's name?" he asked.

"His name is Andrew."

"I don't like it," Ryan answered almost immediately.

Another cut.

"Don't be rude. Remember when you said I was being
rude earlier? Well now you are."

"I'm sorry," he apologised again. "I feel funny."

Another cut. The old lady put the scalpel back onto the
trolley, next to a packet of birthday candles. She picked
them up and tipped the contents of the pack onto the
table next to Ryan's shaking body. She took a hold of
the first candle and put it into the first of the incisions
she'd made. Ryan did his best to watch, laughing as she
inserted the next candle into the next small cut.

"It's like I'm the cake!" he said excitedly.

"That's right." She took a moment from inserting the
candles. "Would you like to blow one out?" she asked.

"Would I?! Yes please!"

"Well good for you." The lady took a plastic lighter
from the trolley and lit the candle closest to the top of
Ryan's chest. It lit after a second and the flame gently
flickered away. Ryan laughed, causing it to shake. "Be
careful," she said, "you don't want to burn yourself."
She helped Ryan lift his head from the table so that his

mouth was closer to the flame. "Don't forget to make a wish," she said, when he was close enough to blow it.

"Done!" Ryan blew the candle. The first couple of blows did nothing but make the flame flicker from side to side. The third blow extinguished it. He laughed, causing the rest to shake once more. "Your son will love it!" he said. "But do you know what you should have done? You should have used some of those magic candles. You know, the ones which go out, only to reignite. That would be brilliant."

"Well, yes, maybe next year."

"I wish I had a mum like you," he slurred. "Mine didn't really have much time for me." He watched as the lady started to carefully insert the candles again - poking them through the open cuts and giving them a little twist to ensure they stayed upright. It would be just their luck, she thought, that he'd move, causing the candles to slip from his body, and end up burning the place down after all the trouble they'd gone to for this party. She inserted the last candle and took a step back to admire her work.

"You look very good," she said.

Ryan smiled, "Thanks."

She walked from the room and down a narrow corridor towards where her husband had gone for a lie down. She turned into the room his bed was in, along with his stolen medical equipment, and froze on the spot. He was there, asleep, cuddled up next to the girl from the gas-station. She was either sleeping or unconscious. Regardless of her mental state, she was definitely not restrained and very naked, with her clothes on the floor by the bed. The old lady went up to her sleeping husband and hit him on the side of his head.

"Wake up!" she hissed. "What the hell is going on here?"

"What?" he sat up and saw what his wife had walked in on. He started to laugh. "It's not what you think. I was trying to help you out and I got tired."

"She is our gift to our son and you couldn't keep it on your pants!"

"Calm yourself, woman!" he pulled himself up from his bed and belted his wife in the face. She stumbled back against the wall, holding her face. Just because she didn't land in a crumpled heap on the floor, it didn't mean his touch didn't hurt. She counted herself lucky. There'd been a time, before the cancer got a hold, where he'd have knocked her to the floor with a single hit - and even that was enough to leave a bruise for a month. He was definitely getting weaker. "I've got so much shit flowing through my veins that even if I wanted to fuck her, I couldn't. Half the reason we're doing this in the first place, remember? The trouble it's caused us, it would have been a damned sight easier had I been able to do it myself. "But I shouldn't have fallen asleep and for that I'm sorry. I am feeling tired and should have known better than to exert myself."

His wife changed the subject, "Where are her party clothes?"

Her husband pointed to the door. Hanging on the back of it was a nice floral, low-cut dress. On a chair, by the bed, was some fresh underwear. Nothing too slutty, plain white silk thong with a matching bra. They didn't want to scare their son off with anything too full on. The woman walked over to the underwear and, starting with the panties, slid them onto the unconscious girl. Her husband watched on as she struggled with the bra. No point asking for his help seeing as he'd already tired himself out by stripping her off in the first place.

"Do you think Andrew will like her?" she asked her husband.

"It doesn't matter what he likes or doesn't like. He needs to do this."

"But it would still be nice if he liked her, wouldn't it?"

The old man shrugged and walked from the room, "I couldn't care less."

The woman sighed and lifted the dress from the back of the door. She removed the hanger and set about getting Christina into it. As she struggled to lift the girl into a sitting position, to put the dress over her head, Christina let out a moan. It wouldn't be long before she was awake and they'd soon be able to get the party started.

SHAW / BRAY

PART TWO

HOW TO MAKE A MONSTER

SHAW / BRAY

CHAPTER FIVE

Pain.
Her face felt as if it had been crushed by a sledgehammer. In a way it had. Her husband's fist being the hammerhead. She heard glass shatter seconds before becoming aware that she had fallen through the coffee table. Blood dripped form her slashed skin onto the carpet, tiny claret beads on a backdrop of brown.

Fistful of her hair, then being dragged, more pain, legs kicking. Richard shouting louder. Another punch in the stomach for good measure, winding her, stopping the screams, stopping the-
Baby
-noise.

Another slap, this time to the other cheek. She could feel her face already swelling, the pain like fire. She was moving again, thrown into the bathroom, losing a shoe, half falling, half sliding, slamming into the side of the bath.

A snap.
Broken collar bone for sure.
Dazed.
Confused.

This isn't supposed to be happening. This wasn't how it was supposed to go. He was supposed to be happy. He was supposed to understand. She had waited four months to tell him. Waited until she couldn't hide the bump anymore. He was supposed to be happy.
Not like this.
Not like this.
Not like this.

He was shouting again, his words fuzzy, hard to understand. Something about betrayal. Something about cleaning her filthy lying mouth. Something about killing the bastard thing inside her.

Oh god.

Panic, hot and prickly, a ball of fire in her gut. But too late to act, too late to do anything.

Another fist, mashing nose into face, a white shard of bloody tooth arcing across the room.

I'm going to die.

She was absolutely certain of it. She had made a huge mistake, an error of judgment which was about to cost her - her life. Right eye almost swollen shut, left blurred but still working.

Able to see.

To see him as he pulls bottles out of the cabinet, see him searching under the sink.

His leering face.

Good god he's smiling.

Handful of her hair, pulling her up.

Legs won't support her though, too weak. Collapses back down, back into the side of the bath. Ribs hurting, collar bone on fire. But not enough to hide the fear. That she can taste, mingled with the blood in the back of her throat. A bitter taste, one she thought she knew but was only really discovering for the first time now, here at the end of her life.

Something in his hand.

A bottle. The smell burning her nostrils, making her flinch away.

Bleach.

Bottle to her mouth, trying to make her drink. Burning as it touches her wounds, more fuel to the fire. She squeezes her lips closed, but he only seems to enjoy it more. Him cackling now like a hyena. A kick to the stomach is all it takes, heavy size ten boot to midriff. She opens her mouth in a half gasp, half scream, then that liquid is being poured in.

She panics.

Can't breathe.

Can't breathe.

She swallows, an instinctive reaction.

Gags, tries to vomit, but he's still pouring, still laughing like some kind of deranged beast.

She swallows again, choking now, bleach coming out of her nostrils.

Still laughing, still enjoying the show.

Gagging, knowing she needs to bring it back up, but he's holding her mouth closed now, massive shovel like hands on her petite face, clamping her jaw closed, screaming at her to swallow.

She does it, the pain now all over her body.

He's got what he wanted. He's satisfied at last. He leaves her lying there on the floor, bleach and blood on black and white tiles.

Am I going to die?

She asks herself the question as the first of the stomach cramps come, then a second question arrives as her body goes into convulsions.

Good god what happens if I live?

#

The doctors said it was a miracle. Tells her she should have died. Of course, any normal doctor would have called the police, would have asked questions about how the broken rib, the chipped tooth, the broken collar bone, the cuts and bruises and the near fatal ingestion of bleach happened. But Richard knew this game. Knew it all too well. He didn't use an ordinary doctor. He went to one of his buddies, one of his drinking pals to get the medical attention she needed. She knew of course it wasn't because he loved her. She wasn't that naïve, not anymore. She knew he needed her to cook and clean, to provide him somewhere warm and wet to stick his shriveled up prick when the mood took him. Either through guilt or realisation he had gone too far, he had agreed to let her have the baby.

That was another miracle. Despite the assault, the baby was still alive. Still growing. Still waiting to be born into whatever future she could give it. She knew for now it would be alright. His rage had been sated. The volcano had blown. He would be calm for a while now.

And what about when he's next ready to blow? What then?

She ignored the question, preferring to stay positive, sure the baby would have a positive effect on them both.

How wrong can a person be?

#

Spring became summer, and on August 10th, 1978, Andrew James Remington was born into the world. As fate would dictate, the less than professional diagnosis of Richards's friend that the child wouldn't show any ill effects from the enforced bleach drinking, the reality was that such an ordeal was never likely to go without consequences. Brain damaged by a combination of the abuse and chemical ingestion, the doctors (real ones this time) told them that it was unlikely that their son would ever live a normal life.

The dreams she had of raising a bright, intelligent being to go and make a difference in the world was shattered. He would never have the mental capacity of anything more than a four year old, they told her, and would need constant care and supervision. She had looked down at him then, simple blue eyes looking out at a world he would never truly understand, his misshapen skull so delicate, so smooth. She looked at Richard then, hoping for a smile, hoping to see a glimmer of love. But he simply stood there by the door, hands folded in front of him, eyes wandering everywhere but looking at his son. She hoped it was guilt, but was fairly certain it was disinterest. She could see he was itching to leave. He had friends to meet, women to screw, and child or no child, he wasn't going to miss it.

"Why don't you go home for a while," she said, not quite willing to admit to herself that the sight of him repulsed her. The way he stood there without any semblance of guilt for what he had done, eyes cold and trouble free.

Even so, he knew a good thing when he saw it, and the opportunity to ditch his family was too good to miss. He made his leave, and at last she was alone.

"We'll leave him," she whispered to her newborn son. "We'll leave him and start a new life by ourselves."

CHAPTER SIX

The idea to leave never became any more than that. A plan, an idea. Fear kept her where she was. Fear and hope. Rather than be the glue to hold them together, Andrews's arrival had served as the catalyst for Richard to increase his intake of drink, and with it the abuse.

He didn't like the way his food was cooked. *(Punch in the face)*

He didn't like the way she looked at the postman when he delivered the parcel. *(Thrown down the steps)*

He wanted coffee instead of tea. *(Broken rib)*

Sometimes there would be no reason, and that was the worst, because she didn't see it coming. He would lash out at will. Once when she was walking to the kitchen, Andrew a drooling two year old in her arms. She nudged his chair with her leg, a perfectly innocent and accidental thing. To him, however, it was the green light to assault her. He'd grabbed her hair, pulling her back towards him; the screams had become part and parcel of the relationship for some time, and now hissing in her ear, telling her she was going to die, telling her that her retard son was going with her.

Scared.

So scared.

She can't hold her bladder, and it lets go, which only adds to his rage.

Hold the baby close. That's the most important thing. Don't let him hurt it.

She repeats it in her head, a mantra, a prayer. She isn't sure which. Either way there will be no mercy from him. There never was.

Punch to the back, agony exploding through her.

Andrew screaming.

Slap to the face, ears ringing, light exploding in her vision.

Andrew still screaming, the simple lack of understanding in his eyes harrowing to see.

Grabbing her arm, fingers squeezing, pinching the skin, digging his thumbs into yesterday's bruises.

At least she can't hear Andrew's screams anymore. Her own are much, much louder.

He stops short at hitting Andrew, and for that she sees a shred of something to hold on to, something to justify staying with him. Something she can build on and put the relationship right.

She isn't so lucky.

He goes out, leaving her a broken mess on the floor. Blood becoming a familiar taste to her now, pain becoming the normal feeling. Andrew crying, abandoned on the floor where he had fallen. She tries to crawl towards him, but the pain is too much, the dizziness too intense. She rests her head on the floor, waiting for the nausea to pass so she can go to her son. She looks up, and he's looking back. Those simple blue eyes bewildered that nobody is coming to his aid.

She crawls, through blood and piss and tears, through agony, through betrayal. She reaches her son, a skinny, wretched bundle on the floor. She strokes the tuft of blonde hair on his head, looking into those simple eyes, relieved that his life will be one without understanding. Although she knows he doesn't understand, she feels the need to explain. To churn out the excuses for the monster.

Daddy didn't mean it.

He loves us really.

It was my fault.

I shouldn't have kicked his chair.

They lay there on the floor, her drifting in and out of consciousness, Andrew cold and screaming.

As soon as she feels able, she stands. She knows the baby needs her. She can smell the mess he has made, but also knows Richard will be home soon, and if the house is still the way it is when he gets back, she will be in trouble. Hating herself for it, she puts the baby in his cot, leaving him in his own stink, leaving him without the milk he was screaming for.

She cleans.

Mops up the blood and urine. Picks up the broken lamp. Straightens the table and chair where they had been dislodged in the scuffle.

I'll get to you soon, I promise I'll get to you soon.

She repeats it in her head, over and over, terrified of Richard coming home before she's finished.

It's slow work, her injuries hinder her, and it's almost dark before she's done. Exhausted, she falls onto the bed, drifting into a semi sleep as her broken body tries to repair the damage.

Andrew isn't crying now. He lay there in his cot in the silence of the desolate house, blue eyes staring at the roof. Cold, wet, hungry, and soiled. He knows nobody is coming.

CHAPTER SEVEN

Spring of nineteen eighty-two.

The Rolling Stones have begun their European tour in Scotland to fantastic reviews, The Falkland's War rages on with more casualties than anticipated, Spanish priest Jose Maria Fernandez Y Khron has tried unsuccessfully to stab Pope John Paul II during his pilgrimage to the shrine at Fatima, and in a large detached house on the outskirts of Indiana, Mary Remington and her two year old son continued to endure their own brand of daily hell.

Richards drinking has gone from every weekend, to every week day night, to every week day, to pretty much all the time. For a while, he scrambled to stay afloat, then lost his footing and fell down that slippery slope. Not only did he lose his footing, he lost his job. Now the respite between eight and six every weekday whilst Richard was at whatever building site he was working on was gone. Instead, he sat in the house, drinking and festering in bitterness and misery. Frustration grew into anger, and was in turn directed towards his family.

Mary crept around the house, terrified to do anything that might trigger his rage. She didn't bother to hide the bruises now, they were too many and frequent anyway. She simply endured the stares of people when she went shopping, ignored the whispers as people pointed at her. Only Andrew looked on her without judgment. He looked at her without prejudice, and why not? As she was the only one who tended to him. She was the only one who got up in the night to change him when he was wet, or feed him when he was hungry.

Never Richard.

He just sat in his chair, waiting for her to step out of line, telling her she was useless, telling her the bastard retard she had spawned had ruined their life and would have been better off if it had died inside her.

The words hurt, in a way doing more damage than the bruises, the lacerations, the broken bones. Hearing him say those things, face twisted into a grimace, sneer across his stubble face.

Like a cancer, he sat in his chair and festered, feeling sorry for himself, growing the hatred which she knew would fall upon her sooner rather than later. Her only respite was when he would go out drinking with his friends, whittling away the money she had managed to save. She couldn't say anything to him of course. She knew well enough by now that she wasn't allowed to question his decisions, and no matter how pressing, she couldn't go against him. She touches her cheek, angry and purple, the payment for asking him what they were going to do for money now, asking how they were going to survive.

His response was heart breaking.

The welfare money for the retard will pay for it.

Never Andrew. Never by his name. Always a put down.

Retard.

Spastic.

Little Bastard.

He called it his retirement fund, his reward for carrying the two of them for the last two years. He would enjoy it and that was that. End of discussion. Mary knew well enough what would come if she questioned it.

Fast forward another year.

Andrew learning to walk, Richard growing more and more violent. Upkeep of the house was becoming impossible. Too much clutter, too much mess, too much time tending to injuries to clean. The house falls into disrepair. The broken gutter she had asked Richard to fix the summer before was still leaking, and had caused damp inside the house, thick black spores growing up the walls. Andrew had developed asthma, leaving him with a constant wheeze and wet cough. He was learning to walk, the cautious toddles of an infant. He still couldn't speak, not in the sense of forming words. He would vocalise, and had already learned through association that his father was a man not to be approached.

Things got worse.

Their stacks of unpaid bills started to have repercussions.

Their power was shut off. Instead of paying the bill, Richard went out and got drunk.

For two weeks, they lived in the cold by candlelight.

It was during that time her first fears were realised. Bored of his constant assault on her, he turned his attention to her son. The occasional bruise on his arm or reddening of the eye.

Still she denied it, told herself it was her imagination, that even he couldn't be so evil.

The next week, she saw for herself that evil itself was living with her.

Andrew toddling on the upstairs landing, gibbering to himself, like her doing whatever he could to exist in such a hostile environment.

Richard getting up after another long night with his friends, bulging stomach hanging over his trousers, hair greasy and filthy.

Walking past Andrew, giving him a nudge as he walks past.

A fall down the steps.

Crying from Andrew, Crying from Mary, neither of them understanding why.

Richard whistling in the bathroom as he purged himself of last night's drink.

Her holding Andrew close, in the back of her mind wondering if maybe Richard was right. Maybe it was the baby's fault, maybe she should have got rid of it.

#

Winter 85.

Things take a darker turn. She thought she had endured everything she would have to, and yet was only at the beginning of what was to come.

Richard, bloated and bitter, his family thin and hungry.

As usual he goes out to wherever he went to meet the friends she didn't know. Leaving her alone, isolated, withdrawn. She never left the house now. Too frightened, too ashamed.

She would know his friends soon enough. Know them all too well.

A little after midnight and he comes home, stinking of booze, cheeks red, and eyes glassy. He has people with him. Two men and a woman. The men she presumes are his friends, his drinking buddies. One a big bear of a man, a mountain of flesh with a thick beard and check shirt. The other, a skinny Asian man with bug eyes and crooked teeth. Both of them stand there behind him, and she knows that they have wives just like her at home, too timid, too frightened to say anything.

She wonders why they are there, who the girl is. She's so young, so pretty, but has that haunted look that Mary recognises too well.

Showing off for his audience, Richard starts to showcase his dominance over her. First with the insults, every answer the wrong one, every response causing more goading.

His friends watching, grinning like loons.

Richard grows into the role.

It's obvious he's the alpha male of this group, and is showing them how he has complete master of his territory.

He tells them how she is timid in bed. How cold and frigid she is, and how tonight it will all change.

Mary looks to the girl, who looks awkward and uncomfortable. Realisation comes then as to why she's here. The denim shorts, the revealing top with a flash of red bra underneath. The makeup caked on to make her seem attractive.

This girl is a prostitute, something which is confirmed by her husband moments later.

He pushes himself on her, keeping an eye on his wife at the same time, making sure she sees, making sure she understands. The girl for her part looks awkward but afraid, and with the transaction already made, has no choice but to go through with it.

This isn't his plan though.

This isn't cruel enough for Richard, not when he has an audience.

He sends the girl towards Mary, telling her what he wants.

Mary isn't like that, she shakes her head and trembles, but dare not say no. she locks eyes with the girl, and sees a flicker of understanding there. She doesn't want this either, but is trapped into her profession, and so more prepared.

Richard goads them on, sneering, nudging his friends as they watch.

Mary and the girl kiss.

It's cold, emotionless, the taste of fear passing between their lips.

Richard tells her what to do. Giving instructions.

Touch her there.

Kiss that part.

Put your tongue in there.

Both Mary and the girl are crying by the end. Both of them naked on the floor, forced to do degrading things to each other. Richard claps his friend on the shoulder, the big one with the beard. He encourages him to get involved. Tells him it's fine.

Even he, the brute of a man has a flicker of doubt, a brief flash of concern as he looks at his friend, perhaps seeing how deeply disturbed Richard actually is for the first time.

He strips, flabby body quivering as he joins in. Probing them both, testing the waters.

Richard cheering and laughing, giving directions, controlling the show.

His other friend with the bug eyes looks uncomfortable. He stands by the door, not sure what he's walked into and less sure how he can get out of it.

How long it goes on for she doesn't know.

She becomes detached from the experience as she is pulled and prodded, violated and groped. She can't hear the grunts, or the cheers, or the well-practiced porn star moans of the girl who is clearly terrified. All she hears is

Andrew, his unanswered cries coming from his bedroom.

Later

They have gone. Friends and whore alike. Richard gone to bed, her laying on the living room floor, naked and quivering, unable to truly comprehend what had happened to her, unable to comprehend what her husband had forced upon her. She retches, the salty aftertaste of the stranger's semen still clogging her throat. Andrew's cries have stopped, they often do these days, especially when nobody goes to him.

She gets to her feet, sore all over, dressing slowly, hands shaking so badly she can barely fasten the buttons on her jeans. In a daze, she walks the filthy house, past the stacks of unwashed dishes, through the mountain of rubbish bags not put out for collection. She stands at the kitchen sink in the dark, staring at the haggard ghost of her reflection in the window.

She doesn't realise what she is doing until she is halfway upstairs, carving knife in hand.

She goes straight to the bedroom, towards the shadow draped mound of her sleeping husband. He's on his back, arms flung to the sides, mouth open as he snored through a fitful sleep.

I may never sleep again.

The thought is the first rational one that has come to her since the assault began.

She isn't sure how long she stands there for. Time doesn't mean anything to her now. She simply watches him, wondering how he can sleep, how he can so easily live with being such a monster. She reaches out, a sliver of steel flashing in the dark. She touches the point of the knife to his throat, telling herself how easy it would be, how simple their lives would be without him.

Just do it.

Finish it.

Make it quick.

The temptation was great, yet she couldn't commit. Hand trembling, blade wavering above his neck. For every reason to do it, another one not to ricochets around her head.

What if he wakes up and sees you?

Don't risk it; you'll end up in prison.

He loves you really.

You can't cope on your own

It was that last that did it. Blinking through the tears, she pulled the blade away, arm hanging limply at her side. Oblivious, Richard snored on, not knowing how close he had come to the end. Mary left the room, shuffling like a ghost around the house, not knowing that the decision to spare his life would turn out to be the worst she had ever made.

The incident was never mentioned again. Richard acted oblivious as if it had never happened, and Mary went along with it because she was too afraid to do anything else. His two friends never again came to the house. She never saw them, nor were they ever mentioned again. She wondered if perhaps they had seen that Richard Remington wasn't the kind of man it was good to become friends with. She looked at him across the table, and understood that evil was real.

She was living with it.

CHAPTER EIGHT

December 86.

Two days until Christmas.

There is no joy in the Remington household though, nothing resembling festive spirit. The house is becoming as worn down and broken as some of its occupants. Floors are filthy, dishes unwashed - not through laziness, but because she simply doesn't have time. Her every waking hour is spent looking after Andrew. She has been trying to toilet train him, and was growing frustrated in her failure. Keeping him in food and nappies was becoming expensive, especially with Richard's refusal to look for work. The savings she had been banking since she first learned she was pregnant had been whittled away to nothing, leaving them on the edge of the poverty abyss.

Mary was thankful that the house was theirs, left to her by her mother, or at least until Richard had beaten her into changing the deeds into his name. She glares at him across the room, dozing in his dog eared chair, stomach hanging out of the bottom of his T-Shirt. She can't decide if she hates him or not. Some days she does, others she remembers how in love they were in the beginning, before she really saw what lurked under the mask she had fallen in love with.

Andrew totters into the room, face slick with drool, clothes filthy. A dirty toe poking out of one of the feet of his mismatched socks. Another little piece of her dies, something she knows she will never recover. She holds out her arms, giving him a sad smile. He comes to her, vocalising in the way he does as he tries to form words.

Gnis

Gnis

Gnis

He repeats it over and over, pointing to the window.

She understands. He wants to see the Christmas lights around the window. They have no tree of course; Richard says they can't afford one.

She wants to ask him how he can afford to drink and smoke every day, but knows she dare not. In fact, even thinking about thinking about it terrifies her that somehow he'll know and punish her for it. She stands, body aching as it always did now. Too many injuries, too many bones left to heal without medical attention. She crosses the room, Andrew following and gibbering. She switches on the lights, a pathetic single string of reds, greens, and yellows strung around the window. They are shoddy at best, and she almost cries at how destitute they are.

Andrew, of course, loves them. He stands there and stares, eyes wide, two toothed smile so pure, so genuine, so in awe. He sees it differently to her. To him, it is beautiful, a rare splash of colour in their life of blacks and greys. To her, she sees the beast they frame, the dim lighting throwing shadows across his bloated, sleeping face.

How she wishes then she had killed him in his sleep, how she wishes she had plunged that knife into his neck, how she wishes she had heard the blade scrape against his spine as she severed his head, hands hot with the heat of his blood as it sprayed their filthy bedding.

He stirs, nothing more than a twitch, but it's enough. Enough to make her scream inside.

Enough to make her draw breath and hold it there like a woman drowning, praying he won't wake up.

Subconsciously, she puts an arm over her son's chest, pulling him close. He stands obediently, already tall for his age, still staring at the lights, still mesmerised as he absently scratches at his head.

Lice again.

She isn't sure how long it will be until she can afford to buy him the treatment. She considers shaving his head, or, as she had seen on TV once, smearing mayonnaise on his head to kill the infestation.

Canca com

Canca com

Canca com

His half formed words cut her deeper still, almost making her feel nauseous.

Santa Come.

That's what he was saying, his face looking to her, grin wide and loving.

How could she live with it? How could she live with knowing that there were no presents for him? Richard wouldn't allow any to be bought. It was one of the few times she had found the courage to stand up to him, for a while at least. She argued how unfair it was, how it wasn't right to deny a child at Christmas.

He stood there in front of her, glaring, cheek twitching, fists balled. She knew she had gone too far, knew she had spoken when she shouldn't have.

He made her pay. Pay in one of the worst possible ways. He beat her until both time and consciousness were vague things. She remembers snatches.

Him throwing her to the floor.

Kicking her in the ribs. Once, twice. A trio.

Deliberately snapping the fingers on her left hand, bending them back until they cracked like kindling, her screams so pure, so far from the pit of her stomach that they seemed to fuel his rage.

She recalls his foot, coming down again and again as he stamped on her head, each blow making her sure she was about to die, then forcing herself to hang on for Andrews's sake.

As always, he stopped when he was too exhausted to continue, flopping down into his chair, the one he dozed in right now surrounded by lights like some kind of monstrous Christmas ornament.

She lay there, unable to move.

Pain.

So much pain all over her body, a living thing, a festering dragon burning her up from the inside. Through her blurred vision, she watched as Andrew had approached his father, crying and confused at what he had just seen.

She wanted to scream, but her mouth was swollen, her jaw likely dislocated. She tried to crawl, but every movement sent her into nauseating spasms. She could only watch as Andrew walked over to Richards's chair, face wet with snot and tears.

Richard looked beyond him at her, half sneering, half grinning. He stood, grabbing Andrew by the arm, roughly dragging him across the room, his feet kicking as his screams intensified. Richard threw him, his tiny body sliding across the kitchen floor and coming to rest against his mother. He leaned on her, looking for comfort, looking for love, but she couldn't reach an arm out to hug him, couldn't speak to offer him comfort. He continued to nudge her, desperate for the protection that she couldn't give.

He glared at them, mother and son in tears at his hand. There was no expression on his face. No sorrow, no remorse. Nothing but a blank mask of absolute neutrality. He went back into the room, swiping the photographs off the mantle as he passed. Glass smashing.

The door slams, and she hears the sound of his truck starting.

Mary can only lay there and shiver, hoping her body finds the strength to heal from the latest bout of injuries. Andrew curls up next to her, sobbing softly, laying on the cold tiles of the floor beside her.

She blinks, back in the present. Body healed for the most part, Andrew back to whatever counted as normal for him.

Still no presents though. Nothing to give him on Christmas morning. Nothing to stop her seeing that wonder filled expression turn to one of utter sadness.

Nothing.

They had nothing.

A single thought came to her, one which she hated herself for even if it didn't make it any less true.

I hope he kills me next time.

CHAPTER NINE

1990.

Another new year, but nothing really changes. The house is nothing more than a hovel, a huge tomb of a place where one woman's dreams for a brighter future have finally died. She sits in the chair opposite her husband. She has aged terribly. Skin lined and leathery from years of abuse, hair dry and lifeless, already greying at the sides. Her eyes look out from beneath a persistent frown. She might chew her lip in thought if not for the cut on it which still hurt. Andrew is twelve and should be on his way to becoming a young man. Sadly, he isn't. He's still unable to control his bowels or his bladder, and can barely speak a few basic sentences.

Richard has taken to sitting him in a garbage bag, tying it up under his arms, taping around the holes cut out for his legs. He's forced to wear it all day, festering in his own stink.

This is Richards's way of teaching.

This is his way of 'teaching the boy a lesson' until he can learn to look after himself.

It's not Andrew's fault of course. He doesn't know any better. He can't control himself. Mary knows the truth, yet she no longer fights, no longer pulls him close like she used to when he was a child.

Andrew falls, landing on his hands and knees. Flies dance and weave around the bag he is forced to wear, interested in the foul contents which had been in there for almost half of the day.

He starts to cry, remaining on all fours.

Mary stands, walking to him in her own crooked way, her spine twisted from a nagging injury when Richard had kicked her in the back hard enough to crack three ribs. She pulls her son to his feet. Tired herself and drained mentally, she doesn't do this with love. She has grown cold, emotionless, even resentful.

She's been thinking a lot about death recently.

At first, the idea repulsed her, however as Richard took more and more from her - when he stopped her having friends or going out of the house without him - she found the idea of ending her existence ever more appealing. It was only Andrew who remained as a stumbling block. She refused to leave him with the monster that was his father.

She looked at him, shuffling around the room, plastered in his own shit. Somehow, despite the things he had endured - the humiliation, the punches and the kicks, the way Richard would sometimes put out his cigarettes on his arms or chest, laughing as Andrew whined in pain - he still had that brightness in his eyes, that complete lack of judgment or hate. It was this which stopped her from going through with her plan.

And planned it she had.

First she would wait until she had put Andrew to bed; his already six foot two frame too big for the filthy mattress on his bedroom floor with yellowed sheets giving little protection from the cold. When he was asleep, she would suffocate him, smother him with his own pillow, waiting until his desperate clawing as he tried to take a breath slowed and eventually stopped. When it was done, she would spend some time with him. Straighten his hair, cover him with a sheet. Make him presentable. Her last act of love before it left her forever.

After that, she would take care of herself. She would be calm, almost excited as she goes to the basement, one of Richard's belts in hand.

She would loop it over one of the pipes down there, sure to select one strong enough to hold her weight. She would spend a few moments there standing on the stool, clearing her head, banishing all thoughts of her husband and thinking only of her son.

She had endured Richard's evil for long enough, and would be determined not to take his sneering face with her into whatever came after.

It was all planned, all arranged.

All she needed was for Andrew to show the first sign of desperation, to show any sign that he was heading the same way she had.

Then, something in Richard changed. Something she saw as a miracle, a thing she had given up all hope for.

His mood lifted. He no longer seemed to be eternally angry, no longer seemed to lash out at her for no reason. He even made an effort to engage her in conversation, although so much time had passed with so little interaction that their discussions were short and awkward.

Even so, it was okay, because he was finally normal. It was like someone had released the tension which festered in him.

She wondered if it was another woman, someone he might have met on one of his nightly jaunts. If it was, she didn't care. As long as she was able to have a little respite. No matter what it was that had happened, she was grateful for it. He was at least making an effort.

Forgiveness came to mind.

Could she, after everything that had happened, learn to forgive the vile acts he had put upon her, or the violence he had started to inflict on his son.

As with all things though, the respite didn't last, and it wasn't too long before the new and improved Richard reverted to his old habits. He became withdrawn, and like any addict, he reverted to what he knew best, which was turning his frustration on his family. Now however, rather than Mary, he concentrated more specifically on Andrew. Around the humiliation, the verbal taunts continued. Richard would call him stupid and ugly, telling him he would be better off dead. Although he still couldn't speak very well, Andrew understood, and cried at his father's words. He took to hiding himself away, pulling his t shirt up over his head to hide his face. When that didn't work, he fashioned masks from paper or card, anything he could find around the house.

Mary was troubled, Richard thought it was hilarious.

Something else changed in Richard. No longer were his days spent sitting in the char by the window, festering and feeling sorry for himself. Now, most of his time was spent in the cellar, clearing out the junk down there, renovating it for reasons he wouldn't share. The one time Mary asked him what he was doing, he told her it was none of her business and gave her that look which told her not to say any more about it.

As 1990 ended on a damp, chilly New Year's Eve, Mary would soon learn the reasons for her husband's behaviour, and become involved in it to the point of no return.

CHAPTER TEN

He called it *Bubuh.*

Mary had given it to him in secret, a toy, his first and only gift given to him when he was ten. It was a doll, a knockoff Chinese Barbie she had found at an old jumble sale. Cheaply made rubbish not meant to last, but cared for and cherished by her son now as much as the day it was given to him.

It's September, a month after his thirteenth birthday, and Andrew is becoming a man in stature if not in mental capacity. At six feet four inches, he towers over his parents. His arms are marked with scabs and scars from the numerous times his father had taken to whipping him with his belt, or putting out cigarettes on his skin. Sometimes he would take a lighter to the boys flesh, cackling as it singed under the flame, as the boy wailed and tried to pull away. Mary simply sat and let it happen, knowing she was powerless to stop it.

Today is a Tuesday, and as usual, Richard and his friends are in the cellar, the sounds of drilling and sawing filling the house. Mary is asleep on the bed; face puffy from yesterday's beating. Andrew is in his room, sitting cross legged on his mattress, paper mask on his face, smaller replica on his toy, his *Bubuh.*

It was filthy and broken, one leg had gone missing, but still he cherished it, stroking its blonde synthetic hair, looking into its plastic face.

He doesn't understand love, not as people are supposed to, but his sheer enjoyment of the toy was as close to that particular emotion as he knew.

He didn't hear his father coming up the steps, his movements masked by the drilling and hammering in the basement. Mary slept through it also. Richard was only heading to the toilet, and had no intention of checking on his son, or caring what he was doing. It was only by chance that he glanced in the boy's hovel of a bedroom as he walked past.

He saw his son.

He saw the doll. The *female* doll that he was playing with.

Rage.

Andrew unaware, stroking the dolls hair, making sure the mask stayed in place.

A balled fist, blindsiding the boy, catching him under the eye, paper mask tearing.

Blood.

Tears.

Richard doesn't stop there. He grabs his son by the throat, not caring that he doesn't understand what is happening. He screams in his face, telling him it's bad enough that he's a retard without becoming a faggot too.

This is Richards's way.

This is his belief.

The boy cowers, eye swollen, blood soaking into the dirty mattress.

Richard's abuse went on, veins bulging out of his neck like steel cord, teeth gritted, eyes glaring.

Another punch.

Nose broken.

Andrew frightened, confused.

Richard taking the toy, standing triumphant by the door.

Andrew wailing, louder than the drilling. Louder than the hammering.

Bubuh

Bubuh

Bubuh

Richard grinning, very deliberate in his actions. He snaps the doll. Pulls torso from leg. Arms from torso. Head from neck.

Andrew screams. A gut-wrenching sound, loud enough to drown out the drilling and the hammering. Loud enough to wake Mary, who charges upstairs.

Wrong place, wrong time.

Richard still angry, and she too eats a punch, bouncing her off the doorframe. He tells her he will deal with her later, and he will. Violating her with the reconstructed doll, hissing in her ear that she needs to be taught a lesson for keeping secrets from him.

Andrew is inconsolable.

He cries all night, and most of the next day. Mourning the loss of his only companion.

Mary hobbles towards him, sore from her ordeal, finally seeing that look in his eyes. The look of resignation, the look of defeat.

She puts a hand out to touch his shoulder, a token gesture. He shoves it away, then picks up the torn remains of his mask and puts it on as he shuffles into the corner, weeping softly.

CHAPTER ELEVEN

The woman was dead.

Mary had gone to bed early the previous night, hoping that by being asleep when Richard came home she would avoid his drunken wrath. She knew of course that he was unfaithful, and he didn't hide the fact that he routinely brought women back with him to the house. When he did, she knew to make herself scarce, hiding in another room and trying not to listen to him grunt as he screwed her.

Last night, however, she had heard nothing, and had awoken to find Richard missing, his side of the bed unslept in. She considered that he might have been injured, perhaps tried his big man act on someone who was more able to handle it. She almost got excited, imagining life without him. She got out of bed, back screaming in agony, bones aching. She crept through the house, pausing to check on Andrew, who was sleeping, lying on his side, knees pulled up towards his chest. She closed the door and went downstairs.

He had clearly come home. The truck was in the driveway, his keys on the table. Fresh bottle of beer on the table by his chair. Clothes, tangled and removed in a hurry were scattered on the rug in front of the fireplace. Tight jeans, pink underwear. Nothing that she would ever own or be able to fit into.

She heard a sound, a grunt from the cellar, then the sound of her husband grunting under his breath, a sound which both terrified her and filled her with an overwhelming sadness that he hadn't met his end whilst on one of his nightly jaunts or drunken drives back home.

He calls to her, barking her name, demanding she go down to him.

She wants to say no, wants no part of the cellar and whatever he's doing down there, however she knows well enough not to disobey, and creeps down the steps, tasting that fear in her throat, having no clue what she would find down there.

The cellar had been transformed into a workshop of sorts. A bench had been installed along on wall featuring what she could only describe as torture equipment. A bench had been constructed, a table designed for the sole purpose of strapping a person to. Thick leather straps were mounted on planks made for human arms and legs. This was only secondary to what she could see in front of her, that bitter flavour of terror tickling her throat and causing her to gag.

The woman was dead.

She lay on the floor, pale and naked, ugly purple bruises around her neck, dead eyes glaring with a fear she knew all too well. Her husband crouched over the body, breathing heavily. They locked eyes. Husband and wife, abuser and abused. She wasn't sure if it was the lighting or the uniquely horrifying circumstances of the situation, but she saw the depravity in him then, the hate in his eyes.

She also understood why she wasn't at all surprised. She had always known he was capable of this. Always knew it would happen sooner or later, she just always assumed it would be her or Andrew that would be laying there dead at his feet, not this poor wretched girl who had trusted a monster and paid for it with her life. He uttered the words she knew were coming and was powerless to resist.

Help me with this.

This.

Not *her*. Not a name.

This.

To him, it wasn't a person. Just a thing, an object. A slab of meat.

The idea that this could be her chance to finally be rid of him didn't enter her head. She was too afraid to say no, knowing that he had passed that point of no return, and that a man like Richard, although dangerous enough, was an entirely different beast now that he had no limits.

Don't do it.

You'll be an accomplice. An accessory.

You will never be free of him

The voice in her head screamed its rational advice, and as desperate as she was to obey it, couldn't bring herself to disobey him, to go against the man who had broken her in every conceivable way.

Then just run.

Go.

Do it later. There will be enough evidence to make sure he never touches you again.

Like before, she was desperate to go along with it, but knew what would happen. If she went against him and left, if she ran screaming from the house about how her husband had finally made the inevitable transition from abuser to murderer, when he knew he would be left with no get out clause, no way to escape the inevitable, she knew what he would do.

He would kill Andrew for the sole reason of knowing it would devastate her. She could imagine it now, his twisted grimace as he told her it was all her fault; she was responsible for the death of their son. It would never have happened if she had just done as he said and helped her.

Mary. I said help me with this.

He was so calm. So composed. She held her breath, and there was absolute silence. She wasn't sure how long it lasted. It could only have been seconds, but felt to her as if hours had passed.

She exhaled, breath fogging in the chilly air. Then, with no other choice, she trudged down the steps and did as she was told.

#

Something in her mind had broken. Together, she and Richard had cut the girl up. Arms at shoulder and elbows, legs at hip and knee. Head removed. Torso halved. Thankfully, she became delirious at what she was doing, acting on some kind of horrified autopilot as she followed his instructions. Richard on the other hand was calm, a picture of composure as he went to the body with his handsaw, steel on bone sounding horrifically loud in the silence of the cellar, the wet tear of flesh and muscle cutting through her like fingernails on a chalkboard. When it was done they bagged her up.

It.

It. Don't refer to it as a person. She reminded herself. It will make it easier.

They put it into bags, so much meat in the same brand of garbage bag Richard forced Andrew to wear instead of diapers. They waited until after dark and then had gone out of the city, into the wilderness. Richard saying he knew a place. A place where they could bury it deep.

It.

Mary wondered what her name had been.

They reached the spot, an abandoned scrub of wasteland, a few sick looking trees for cover. This would be her (it's) final resting place. This is where she (it) would spend her (its) eternity. They dug a grave, a shallow pit in which to toss the bags. No ceremony. No farewell. A clinical operation. Something fitting of a man like Richard. They worked in silence, her horrified, him indifferent. She realised this wasn't the first time he had done this. Not by a long shot. She wondered how many he had killed, how many lives had been lost in order to spare hers. She couldn't decide if she was more guilty or relieved, then decided it didn't matter. She was alive, and if it meant a stranger would have to die, then she thought she could live with it.

#

It all made sense.

She wasn't quite sure how or why, perhaps the release of committing murder was all Richard needed to bring a sense of normalcy into his life. His mood once again changed for the better. Gone was the cloud of anger and frustration, the bitterness and self-pity. In its place was the man she thought she was marrying all those years ago.

A man who was gentle, attentive, interested in engaging in conversation. He even bought her flowers. Mary wondered if this was it, if this was what she had been waiting for all these years, if this was what he had needed to let off some steam and give her and their son the love the craved.

Like all things, and as history had already proved, this particular leopard wasn't so easily able to change its spots. For a month and a half, Mary lived in absolute happiness, when out of the blue, he came home from

155

work, stinking of booze and the cheap perfume of whichever cheap slut had fallen for his charms.

He sat in his chair, the Richard of old, brow furrowed in thought, massive hands splayed on the arm rests of the chair. At this point, she would have expected a beating, maybe for something or more likely for nothing at all. This time though, he didn't attack. He simply turned towards her and locked his cold eyes on hers.

We have to do another.

Not him.

Us.

We.

She shook her head, telling him she couldn't go through with it. Pleading for him to reconsider.

He grins at her, the smile of a crocodile or maybe a rabid dog.

He tells her she's already involved. Delights in explaining how she is an accessory. How by helping him dispose of the last one, she's as much a part of it as he is.

This is his way.

He manipulates.

Twists the truth and intertwines it with his own deluded fiction so that even she wonders if he might actually be right.

She starts to believe. Starts to see what few options she has.

He knows her, this wife of his.

Knows her ways.

Knows how she thinks.

Knows he needs something extra. Something to really convince her that she has no choice.

The answer is easy.

It's a six foot five child in an adult body.

He tells her how if she doesn't help, they might be arrested. Both sent to prison.

Tells her Andrew will be put into a home for retards. He will die alone and hating her.

He's very careful about this.

Very deliberate in including her in the consequences of their actions.

He turns on the sympathy, reaches out and grasps her hand in his, feels it trembling and smiles inside.

I won't let anything happen to you, he tells her, knowing that if it came down to it, he would gladly sacrifice her to save his own skin.

You're my girl. I love you.

He knows this will work, and almost feels sorry for how easy it is when he sees the light in her eyes at those three simple words.

Words which have no meaning to him.

To her though, they mean everything. He forces a smile. A mask. Nothing more.

She comes to him, nodding, telling him she will do whatever he wants. She hugs him, sobbing into his neck.

Stupid bitch.

He knew all along how it would go.

Planned it all meticulously.

Now the game can begin.

He holds her at arm's length. Still playing the game. Still wearing that mask.

He tells her she won't need to see him do what he needs to do. Only help him after.

She asks if he will do it in the cellar again, and he nods. Tells her that's why he prepared it. Reassures her she won't have to do anything until after. Until it's time to clean.

What else can she do but agree?

She sits there as he stands, pulling on his green jacket. Tells her he isn't sure when he'll be back.

He kisses her on the head.

Cold lips.
Warm skin.
The lips of a monster on the skin of a willing victim.

CHAPTER TWELVE

They become more frequent, his hunts.

She falls into a routine of helping him. Usually, she sits upstairs with Andrew whilst Richard takes them to his room in the cellar. On other occasions, she hears it all, every scream, every beg for mercy.

She knows this well.

She lived it for so long it will never leave her.

And yet, since their new arrangement, he barely touches her. Granted, he still beats her on occasion, but nowhere near as often as he used to.

It's August 4th, 1991.

Andrew is growing at an alarming rate, at least in the physical sense. Mentally he still struggles to string simple sentences together, or to really understand what kind of awful bastard of a world he has been born into.

Richard had come home with one of his victims, this time a man called Victor. He was young. A student.

Richard had brought him back to the house, playing up to the idea that he too was gay, enticing the younger man in. Just close enough to strike.

He never stood a chance.

Mary sits in her chair, listening to those awful sounds from the cellar. Listening to her husband do the one thing which made him happy.

Tonight, she is distracted by Andrew.

He's excited tonight, pacing around the room. He's so big, so broad.

He walks to the cellar door, putting his ear against the wood, perma-grin dripping with drool as he listens.

She knows that expression.

He likes it.

A year ago it would have filled her with horror.

Now she wonders if having him help might make the work of disposing of the bodies easier.

#

It makes the news.

Victor Horrowitz, missing student and much loved friend. Public appeals for his safe return. Richard watches with the faintest of smiles, Mary haunted by the photograph on screen of the man who lay dead in their cellar.

Later they dispose of the body.

The three of them.

Richard insists on bringing Andrew along. Says they can use his strength to help dig.

She watches horrified as he sits on the back of the van, grinning and gibbering over the body. He keeps touching Victor's eyes, prodding at them and gurgling with laughter.

Bubuh

Bubuh

He says, looking at her for approval.

Somehow she swallows her scream.

#

They bury the body. Deeper this time. Andrew starts to get upset, so she makes it a game. He gargles and laughs, having the time of his life, not understanding what was going on, or how fundamentally wrong the entire situation is.

Richard looks at him, something resembling an emotion. She doesn't think its love. That's an emotion she doesn't feel he's capable of, but it's something close. He says something that she doesn't quite catch. She asks him to repeat it, hoping she misheard.

He's a chip of the old block, isn't he?

She wants to scream, and then she realises he's looking at her, waiting for a response, expecting her to answer.

The scream threatens to eject itself from her throat, but she somehow manages to swallow it. She looks at her sun, who is kneeling in the dirt, patting down the earth on the shallow grave.

It almost escapes again, that scream in fear of her son becoming the same kind of monster as his father.

She manages a weak nod, hoping it suffices.

He stands there for a moment, shovel in hand, breath pluming in the chilly night air. She sees the twin pinpricks of moonlight reflected in his eyes, and knows he's analysing her, assessing his next move. She wonders if he's deciding if she's more trouble than she's worth, and can't help her eyes falling to the shovel in his hands.

He could kill me right here.

She has contemplated this before of course, but that was always at home. Never out here, never in his domain. She wonders if he even recognises her, or if he just sees a body. A woman to take out his rage and aggression on.

She waits, holding her breath, the only sound their son's cooing as he plays in the dirt.

Richard exhales, sliding his grip on the shovel to the middle to easier carry it.

161

Come on. Let's go home.

With those words, the moment is gone, and she can breathe a sigh of relief. She knew it would all be okay, for a while at least. Until his mood changed and he felt compelled to go through the whole process again.

CHAPTER THIRTEEN

Horrowitz had been taken on the 4th, killed on the 5th, and buried on the sixth. Mary was sure it would be the end of it for a while at least. She was prepared to enjoy one of those all too brief periods of relative peace and joy.

As was the way in her life, it wasn't so simple. Just four days later, on a hot, sticky night where there was no wind of any description, Richard had leaned forward in his chair and looked at her. She hadn't seen him at first. She was busy trimming Andrew's hair as he sat cross legged in front of her.

She caught him watching her, and stopped, scissors poised.

I'm going out for a while. Don't wait up.

She knew of course what this meant. It wasn't the ordinary way he would announce he was going out. This meant something else altogether.

She asked him why another, why so soon.

His answer was chilling in its simplicity.

Because I can.

Conversation over, he stood and shrugged into his jacket, giving them a last look as he stood by the door. She watched him go, listening to the throaty growl of the engine of his truck as he started it and reversed out of the driveway and off to wherever he intended to select his next victim.

She made sure she didn't hear it.

She put Andrew to bed and had gone at the same time herself, putting cotton balls in her ears, curling up tight in the bed and doing all she could to fall asleep. She couldn't do so naturally, and relied on an ever expanding cocktail of sleeping pills and painkillers to send her away. She had taken an extra dose, enough to make sure she wouldn't wake up to witness or hear his depraved acts.

#

Golden bars of sunlight woke her, bringing her from a groggy landscape of half remembered night terrors. As usual, Richard's side of the bed was still neat and tidy, a sure indication that he had found what he had set out to find. She clambered out of the bed, pushed her feet into tatty slippers and pulled on her ancient, dog eared dressing gown. She went downstairs, not able to remember the last time she had slept later than eight, never mind until almost ten. She was surprised Andrew hadn't woken her. He was a demanding child and she felt a pang of guilt for sleeping so long.

She went downstairs, feeling the prickle of fear at the base of her spine.

The house was empty.

She should be able to hear Andrew playing whilst Richard sat in front of the television. She looked around the over cluttered living space. TV switched off. Andrew's paper mask abandoned on the sofa.

She stood there, frozen on the threshold of the room, chewing her thumb raw.

Andrew?

She croaked the word, the sound of it incredibly loud and sharp in the silence of the house.

A noise. Richard calling out to her. Beckoning her.

She knows there is only one reason.

She knows where he is.

She walks to the cellar, heart like a trip hammer, knowing she is already in deep, far, far too deep.

She opens the door, goes down the stairs.

There is a girl.

Blonde, pretty.

Not one of his usual sluts.

She's dead.

Eyes open, tongue bloated and protruding slightly from a partly open mouth.

Richard smiling, knife in hand, poised ready to cut.

So proud.

So happy.

She wants to scream.

Wants to run.

Then she sees Andrew.

He stands beside his father, stroking the girl's hair, dopey grin on his face. He speaks, his voice sharp and crisp in the bare walled space.

My Bubuh

My Bubuh

Richard grins.

There he is, she thinks to herself. There is the proud father she always hoped he would be. But not like this. Not this way.

I think he likes her.

Richard says, ruffling the boy's hair.

Andrew is oblivious. He continues to stroke the dead girl's face.

My Bubuh

My Bubuh

Mary can see his confusion. She resembles the doll. The one thing he had and cherished that was taken from him.

She turns and runs back up the steps. She can't handle this. Can't handle it at all.

She needs air, needs space. Needs to get away from them both.

Richard sees it her eyes and gives chase, tossing the knife on the dead girl's chest.

She bursts out of the cellar, charges through the kitchen and to the front door, fumbling to unlock it, knowing she has to stop this before Andrew becomes the mirror of his father.

Her face mashed into the wood.

Nose broken again.

Thrown on the floor.

Richard glaring, eyes on stalks, fists balled.

She knows she's made a mistake, knows that in this phase, Richard isn't a man likely to stop at a beating. She tries to scramble to her feet, but he kicks them from under her, sending her crashing back to the floor.

She knows what's coming, and only hopes he kills her quickly.

A foot to the stomach, knocking both fight and air out of her.

This would have been enough. This would have been sufficient to stop her trying to run, but she knew Richard all too well. He liked to make his point.

Another foot in the same place, delivered with a venom she had never experienced before. Her whole body seems to stop, she can't breathe, can't move.

This is it. She thinks. This is how it's going to end.

Handful of hair and he's dragging her up.

Slammed into the wall, eyes wide, his massive hands on her throat. Squeezing.

He's grinning, and she wonders if this is what they saw before the end, those victims of her husband the killer. Her vision begins to dim, legs start to buckle. Even the sting of pain can't keep her awake. She sees something else then, something behind Richard.

Their giant son.

He grabs Richard and throws him with little effort across the room. He crashes into the coffee table, shattering it under his weight.

No! Andrew screams.

They both stare at their son. Husband and wife, and for once, they have some common ground. They look at each other, identical expressions on their face.

Andrew is wearing the girl's face.

The cuts are rough and amateurish, but the intent is clear.

His bubuh Mary thinks.

She glances back at Richard, and he at her.

Both of them know that his days of beating her are done, as are any hopes of her ever trying to flee. Her son is involved. Her poor, lonely son who wanted only companionship had found it in his father's sick obsession.

Guilt told her she wouldn't deny him again, and if that meant helping Richard with his needs, then she would do it.

They watched as Andrew shuffled back down towards the cellar, holding the bloody homemade mask to his face, leaving Richard and Mary alone and stunned in the living.

CHAPTER FOURTEEN

Ten years pass and the cycle of depravity continues.

Mary's spirit has long been broken. Her son is a giant of a man, seven feet of childlike curiosity. Her protector from an abusive husband, who hasn't laid a finger on her since that day when everything changed. She sits in a chair, now in a new space, a warehouse where they live, a space where Richard has devised a new game to entertain both himself and his son.

Andrew had become quite adept with a sewing needle, and he shuffles into the room, ducking under the doorframe. He sits opposite her and starts to eat his sandwich, dead eyes shining from beneath the leathery mask of human skin he wears. He rarely takes them off.

She watches him eat, listens to the wet smack of his lips as he devours his food.

She sighs and lights a cigarette, any love or bond with her boy long gone.

She looks at the letter on the table, the one addressed to her husband and feels a surge of anger.

The letter says his cancer is in remission.

She knows it doesn't mean he's cured, but it has bought him more time. She thinks back over the years at the spate of abductions and murders, and can't help but be grateful for the times when Richard had been too ill to perform. Those times when he was sick from his chemotherapy and couldn't indulge his urges were blessed gaps in the constant horror.

She thinks that if God exists, he has a sick sense of humour for allowing a monster like her husband a second chance to live.

He's out there now, looking for a victim, looking for someone to bring back.

She wonders where it all went wrong, and can't remember when she went from a mother protecting her son to a lonely isolated woman.

Bitterness and hatred had grown in her for them both, and not for the first time, she wishes she had died the day Richard made her drink the bleach, or that at least Andrew had.

She watches him eat, jam all over his mask as he crams the sandwich in.

She hates him.

He reaches out a massive, dirty hand to grab his glass of milk and knocks it over, spilling it on the table.

He cries.

She stands and hits him on the side of the head, twisting the mask.

Stupid little cunt. She hisses.

He lowers his head and sobs.

She goes to him then, holding his head to her chest, stroking his hair.

It always goes like this. The mood swings. The love hate relationship.

They hear Richard's van rolling up to the building. Mary goes back to her chair and sits, eyes cold, emotion long beaten out of her.

Andrew stands, pacing and agitated. She can see his mouth behind his mask. He's grinning, he's happy.

My Bubuh

My Bubuh

He repeats over and over again, going to the window to check it's his father, then running downstairs to help him bring in their latest victim.

She doesn't move. She simply sits there and smokes, knowing that this is her life, this is how it will always be. A dysfunctional alliance born from violence and hatred.

Her eyes go to the letter on the table, and she only hopes that one day the cancer would find the strength to complete the task she couldn't and finish off her monster of a husband. Until then, she would continue to help them, knowing she was too far in to do anything else, and too broken to ever lead anything resembling a normal life. She stubs out the cigarette in the overstuffed ashtray and stands, wincing at the protest in her aching body. Then she sighs and shuffles downstairs to help.

PRESENT DAY

SHAW / BRAY

CHRISTINA

1.

I was shaking despite my best efforts not to. I wanted to remain calm, not because I believed them when they kept saying I was going to go free - that I was going to be okay and permitted back to my daughter again - but because I didn't want to give them the satisfaction of knowing how scared I was.

I had woken in a new room. It looked as though I was still in the same building. More of a stench up here, filling the rooms, if that's at all possible. My hands were still restrained above my head though, higher up this time - no way I can reach my wrists with my teeth from here. Despite feeling light-headed, I instantly realised I was wearing new clothes. My own clothes were folded, neatly, on the chair next to where I lie as though - at some point - I'm going to be permitted back into them again; a false hope put in my head to put me at ease I wonder? There was some medical equipment by the seat - some kind of drip - and a window on the far wall, boarded by a piece of wood.

Use the chair to break through the wood.

I feel sick; not sure whether it's because of the smell lingering in my nostrils or because of that crap he'd used on me to knock me out again. Despite feeling unwell, I was trying to remain as quiet as possible. I didn't want them knowing I was awake yet. I didn't want them coming to get me. The longer I wait, the more chance there is of the cops getting here.

Please let the CCTV have been fixed.

I could hear voices outside of the room. I'm not sure how close they are, I just hope they're not headed this way. My hopes are dashed as the door swings open and crashes against the wall. It's the old lady. The old man is standing next to her.

"How are you feeling?" she asked me. The tone in her voice suggested she cared but I know she doesn't. She only cares about her family, not the people brought in to please them.

"My head hurts," I told her. It does. It's pounding hard and heavy. Another side effect from the crap he keeps putting me to sleep with?

"You're probably thirsty," the old lady said. "It's important to stay hydrated and - despite trying to keep the place tidy - it's quite dusty in this building, especially downstairs, which doesn't help." She stepped into the room. The old man lingered in the corridor beyond the doorway. "Now, it's nearly time for the party but before I take you through, I'm going to have to go through some ground rules, okay?"

"When can I go home?" I asked. So much for trying to remain calm, as a tear welled up in my eye.

"Soon," she said.

"My daughter will be worried. Can I at least call her? Please?"

"I'm sorry but that's not possible."

"I'll do whatever you want me to, I just want to call her and let her know I am okay. Please. I won't say anything about where I am or what is happening. I'll keep it short. I just want to tell her that I love her and that I'll see her soon. Please. You're a mother, you must understand."

"Ssh," she raised her finger to my lips. It was cold, boney.

Bite it off.

174

She pulled her finger away. "Even if I was going to let you use a phone, I'm afraid it's just not possible. We do not have a phone-line connected to the property."

"You must have a mobile… Please! I'm begging you!"

"You know my answer and that will be the end of it. Now, as I was saying before you so rudely interrupted me, we need to go through the ground rules before the start of the party."

"I don't want to go to any fucking party," I hissed.

The woman slapped me hard in the face, stinging my cheek and causing my eyes to well up more so than they already had. "Behave yourself. You are a lady, you shall act as such. My son will not go with a tramp, do you understand me?"

Tell her to fuck herself.

I went to open my mouth again only for her to slap me harder this time.

"A simple nod will suffice. Do you understand?"

I nodded.

"Now it's important you listen," she continued as though nothing had happened. "You've seen how easy it is to upset Andrew. We don't want him getting upset on his birthday, especially seeing as it's such a big day for him. With that in mind, we're going to take you through to the party room and give you some time alone in there to adjust to your surroundings and the people you'll be with…" the bitch continued.

Wait? Other people? Maybe someone will help me?

"If you try anything, you will never see your family again. Furthermore, as per my threat downstairs, we will fetch your daughter and she can be the guest of honour instead. Do you understand me?"

I nodded again, scared to open my mouth. The old lady smiled. I'd give anything to wipe that smile from her face. Hit her so hard that she loses some teeth.

"We have put a lot of effort into this and we don't want anything to ruin it, just as I'm sure you wouldn't want anything, or anyone, to ruin a party thrown for your daughter. Am I right?"

I nodded again.

"Good." She turned to her husband, "Have you got the wheelchair?"

He nodded and pulled it into my line of sight; a tatty old chair, the sort you'd find in a hospital ward. I guessed that too was stolen. The old lady leaned across to the ropes around my wrists and started to fiddle with the knots.

Push her away and jump through the wooden board in front of the window.

The first rope came away easily whereas the second took a little fiddling to get undone. Despite what my brain told me, I didn't move when I was finally free to do so. The woman pulled the chair into the room and told me to sit on it.

"We're going for a ride."

"I'm fine to walk."

"Sit."

I took a seat on the wheelchair. She spun the chair around so we were facing the doorway, and pushed us out into the corridor. The corridor looked the same as the one I'd run down when I first got myself free from my restraints. For all I know it could have been and I was still downstairs, just in a different room. I'm so disorientated I could be anywhere. The old man led the way through to a large room; a table in the centre of it, eerily surrounded by mannequins. More windows, boarded up, and birthday banners hung around the room.

My heart skipped a beat when I saw the other prisoner, from downstairs, as the table's centre-piece; his chest covered in gore, candles sticking from his tissue, his head to the side with a pool of sick leaking out and his skin so pale and clammy.

"What the hell is this?" I felt my heart pulsating in the back of my throat as I realised the bodies around the table weren't mannequins but rather dead people; people previously reported as missing in the papers I sold in the gas station. "What the fuck is this? You're fucking sick!" I started shouting as tears of fear streamed down my face. I went to get up off the chair but the old lady pushed down heavily on my shoulders, pinning me to the chair. I struggled. By God I struggled under her grip.

Break free, make a run for it.

I stopped when I realised the old man was pouring a clear liquid from a brown bottle into a dirty-looking rag.

He'll put you to sleep. Can't do anything whilst you're asleep.

I put my hands up, "I'm sorry. You don't need to knock me out. I was just startled, that was all!"

The old lady relaxed her grip of my shoulders a little. I didn't try and make a run for it, despite the want. Now isn't the time. There'll be other times.

Will there?

I hope so anyway. If I carry on now, though, they'll knock me out and I won't be able to do anything. I need to remain conscious. I need to remain alert. Wait for an opportunity and snatch it. I was wheeled over to an empty chair next to one of the dead bodies.

The stench!

"That's your seat," the mother told me.

Reluctantly I sat next to the dead body wondering who it was when it was alive.

Don't think about it.

The old lady stepped out from behind the wheelchair and pointed to the two chairs opposite where I was seated. "These," she said, "will be where my husband and I will sit. The chair at the end the table is where Andrew will be sitting. He may be a little nervous to begin with so I ask you to be patient with him, okay?"

I nodded.

Fuck you.

She turned to her husband, "What do you think? Should we fetch him?"

The old man was staring at me, a look of hatred in his eyes that made me feel both unwelcome and also violated. I shifted uneasily in my seat, accidentally knocking the body next to me. It slumped forward and banged its head on the table, causing me to jump and the other prisoner to groan.

He's alive? I thought he was dead.

The old lady made a funny 'tut' noise in her head as she adjusted the position of the corpse so that it was sitting back upright.

"I'm sorry," I told her, "it was an accident."

"Just try and be more careful. We've gone to..."

I interrupted her, "a lot of trouble, I know." She stared at me, seemingly irritated I'd dare to finish her sentence. I quickly changed the subject, "I love what you've done to the place. I'm sure Andrew will too."

"What are you talking about? It's horrible. But this is to his taste and that's all that matters." She looked back to her husband, "Did you want me to get him or will you?"

"I'm pretty tired," her husband said. He walked over to one of the empty seats and pulled it away from the table before taking his seat. "Would you mind?"

His wife shook her head, "No. Keep an eye on our guest." She didn't wait for her husband to acknowledge her before she turned and walked from the room, closing the door behind her. A split second later and I hear a lock click shut.

Damn.

It was just me and the old man. The old man who was still staring at me, unblinking. I took the opportunity to try and find out why I was here. All they kept saying was that I was to be the guest of honour but surely that should be their son? It was his birthday, after all.

"Why am I here?" I asked.

"You're the…"

"Guest of honour, I know. I was told."

"Then you know why you're here."

"No, I don't. If it's his birthday then surely your son should be the guest of honour."

The old man laughed, "He doesn't even know what day it is. He's useless. A waste of oxygen…"

I was shocked to hear the father speak of his son in such a way, "He's your son."

"He's a broken sperm. He shouldn't be alive. If it weren't for… my condition. He wouldn't be. He's only here because I need him."

"If that is how you feel, why are you going to all of this effort?"

"To make him feel relaxed for what's to come. Besides, none of this was my idea. You were my idea. But this, this party - that's nothing to do with me. That's all to do with her. His mother. She loves him. There's something very unconditional about the love of a mother. You're a mother so I am sure you understand but - when a father sees his son as a disappointment… It's quite easy for the father to turn their back to them. It's quite easy to disown them and pretend they don't exist."

"What's to come?" I asked, picking up on what he said. Why would his son need to be relaxed for what was to come? What were they planning? I asked again, "What's to come?"

"His present."

"Which is?"

The old man smiled. I went to say something when the lock on the door clicked once more. I felt an uncomfortable surge of adrenaline through my veins as the door opened. The son wasn't there though, it was just the old lady. She was standing there, a look of anger on her face. Or was it disappointment? Her husband turned to her, "What is it? Where's Andrew?"

She didn't answer him. Her eyes were fixed on me; a look which made me even more uncomfortable - not that I thought that to be possible.

"What is it?" I nervously asked.

"Where's his birthday card?"

"What?!"

"It's his party," she said, "you needed to bring a card. That's what you do at parties."

"Well did anyone else bring one?" I couldn't believe what she was saying.

"Of course not. They're dead."

"What about him?" I pointed to the unconscious body of the man lying on the table.

"He's the cake. Do you often get birthday cards from your cakes?" she hissed.

I wasn't sure whether she was joking. A sick joke to make me feel more on edge? What the old man said about his son, was that too a sick joke to get a reaction? Maybe a way of making me feel sorry for the son? Is that what he was trying to do? Why would he do that, though? Why would he care? "Where is his fucking card?" she asked again; so much venom in her voice.

180

"I didn't get him one!" I said, panicking.

"What kind of person comes to a party without a card?" she stormed across the room and started hitting me upside the head. I put my hands up to protect myself but - despite her age - she was moving like lightening and half of the blows she threw landed where she intended. I screamed out as her husband just sat opposite us, laughing. She suddenly grabbed my head and slammed it down onto the table with a heavy thud which sent shockwaves through my entire brain and caused my vision to blur. I cried out - both in pain and for her to stop. She slammed my head down again, and again…

2.

Open your eyes and it will all have been a dream; a terrible nightmare. You'll be in bed, with Greg. Courtney will be in the other room, laughing at something on the television. Greg will tell you to ignore the alarm ringing from your mobile phone. He'll tell you to call in sick to work and he'll cuddle into you. Of course you won't phone in but you'll enjoy the cuddle for a few minutes more before having to get up. All you have to do is open your eyes.

I opened my eyes. My head was leaning on a table; a table stretched out before me with corpses sitting either side. A deranged version of The Mad Hatter's Tea Party. I'm not at home then. It wasn't a bad dream brought on by reading horror just before I turned the light out.

"You could have killed her and then where would we be?" the old man was berating his wife for what she'd done to me. I blinked hard to clear the stars from my vision. I slowly sat up straight. The whole room was spinning violently.

Make it stop, I want to get off.

"Well she's awake so we're fine."

Someone was crying in the room; the sound came to my right. I turned to look; the other prisoner was awake. I couldn't see his face from where I was sitting but I could see his body shaking from where he was weeping.

He's awake then.

"Here, sign this!" the old lady slammed a blank card down in front of me, along with a pen.

Take the pen and slam it into her neck.

I picked the pen up with a shaking hand and pressed it against the card, choosing to ignore the little voice in my head, "I don't know what to write," I said.

"Happy Birthday would be a good start," she replied. "To Andrew, Happy Birthday, Lots of Love and whatever your name is."

"Christina."

"What?"

"That's what my name is. My daughter's name is Courtney and my boyfriend's name is Greg."

The old man laughed, "Is Greg a forgiving man?"

I wanted to tell the old man that he wasn't. I wanted to explain that Greg was going to take great pleasure in hurting both of them for what they'd put me through. The little voice in my head told me to keep quiet though.

Keep quiet or else they'll hurt you again.

"Just sign the card," the old lady spat, giving me a way out of having to answer her husband. I wrote what she'd told me too. There was no point in writing anything but.

"Why did you choose me?" I asked. The town I lived in wasn't small by any stretch of the imagination. I could walk down the street and pass no one that I'd recognise. The chances of this happening to someone I knew were so slim. What did I do to deserve this?

"Because we'd heard you mouthing off at the gas station, saying you'd knew it was us."

"What? When I was talking to my friend Jessie?"

"If that's what her name is," the old lady shrugged.

"We were just talking. I was giving your vehicle a story, I often do that with cars - or people - when I'm at work. It passes the time!" I burst into tears at how something so trivial, so stupid, could have landed me in so much trouble. "I didn't know it was anything to do with you! I picked your vehicle because it was a van so easy to hide bodies! I didn't know!"

The old lady started to laugh, "Well now you do." She turned to her husband, "Let's try this again, I'm going to get Andrew. Keep an eye on her and - if it's not too much trouble - feel free to light the birthday cake."

"Birthday cake?! It's a human fucking being!" I yelled.

The old woman snapped, "Calm yourself before Andrew gets here," she said. "You know the rules, unless you'd prefer we did this with your daughter."

"No. I'm sorry."

Keep them away from Courtney.

The old lady turned and left the room. The lock clicked. The old man stood up and walked over to the quivering body of the other prisoner. He shook his head when he looked at the state of him, "How anyone could like this is beyond me. Further proof - if it were ever needed - that my son should be dead."

"If you feel that way, why don't you kill him?" I said. I couldn't hide the venom in my voice.

"This poor lad or my son?"

"Either."

"He needs to be alive because my son only eats from them whilst they're alive... Well... He eats from them when they're freshly dead but..."

What?

"...And I need my son if my name is going to continue through the ages. I'm dying, I don't have any other children." He shook his head, "It doesn't matter. Let's light the cake!" He fished in his pocket and pulled out a plastic lighter.

"Please help me," the man on the table was still crying. I felt bad for him but there was nothing I could do. Was their son really a cannibal? Was he really going to eat him? No. It has to be fake. The whole thing is fake. Some kind of sick prank by one of my friends? Or one of those extreme experiences? I've read about them; extreme horror mazes where you're in there until the very end and no matter how much you shout and scream, no one will let you out until you see it through. Maybe this is one of those? One of my friends organised it for me because they know I love horror? Maybe even Greg organised it with Courtney's help? No. I'm reaching out. I'm being stupid. They wouldn't put me through this just because I enjoy horror. This takes things too far. It has to be real. The old man walked back over to his seat and sat opposite me, placing the lighter on the table. I looked at the man on the table. All of the candles were lit. This can't be for real.

I jumped at the sound of the door lock clicking back round. The door opened and the old lady came in, leading her son by a collar around his neck. He bent down as he walked in. As soon as he saw the table he made a grunt of appreciation and jumped up and down; shaking the whole room in the process. One of the candles toppled from the man's body and landed next to him. The flame went out. In the split second it happened, I'd hoped it would have set the whole building ablaze so I'd have a chance to escape.

"Calm yourself," the mother told her son. She closed the door behind them.

I'd forgotten how big he was.

"This is your seat," he sat next to me, at the head of the table. He looked first at the man with the candles sticking from him before turning to me. More grunts of excitement as he rocked from side to side. His mask had changed now from the time I'd seen him earlier; it looked as though a child had painted it white with black rings around the eyes, red patches on the cheeks and big, red lipstick over the decaying lips. I turned away from him, disgusted. The old lady sat opposite me.

"Don't you have something for Andrew?" she asked me.

She was referring to the card. Where did they even get a spare birthday card from anyway? Did they pop to the shops at some point and get it on the off-chance they needed a second? Is it one that had meant to go to another home and simply been forgotten about until now?

"Did you not hear me?" she snapped. Both her son and I looked to her. Her eyes were fixed upon me; burning hatred. Her son followed her gaze in time to see me smile.

Don't upset him.

"This is for you," I said, handing over the birthday card.

He snatched it from my hand and howled with excitement. Both a gesture, and a noise, that made me jump.

Don't let him know you're scared.

"Happy Birthday," I told him.

He was sniffing the card, unsure of what to do with it.

"You open it," I said. "It's a card."

He looked at me with suspicious eyes. I carefully reached out and took the card from him. He grunted in response and for a second time when I tore it open. I pulled the card from the envelope and handed it to him, "Here you go."

He looked at his mother and father, shocked that a card had magically appeared from a brown envelope. He howled again and snatched it back from me, opening it up in the process - purely by accident.

"It says 'To Andrew, Happy Birthday, Lots of Love Christina'," I told him.

The old lady smiled as her son grunted with excitement, "Well isn't this wonderful!" She clapped her hands together, startling me again.

186

Hold it together. They said I can go home after the party.

I looked over to the man with the candles, he was still sobbing and the candles were still shaking. I hated what I was about to suggest but I didn't have any other choice. No one was coming for me; I was trapped here for as long as they wanted me. They said I could go after the party and, although I doubt it was the truth, there's nothing else I have to believe in. It's clear God doesn't exist. Their possible lie is all I have and if I were to get this party wrapped up, we needed to cut to the cake. "Are we going to cut the cake?" I asked.

Both parents looked up to me, surprised I'd suggested it. I guess they thought - when the time comes - I'll be the one kicking up a fuss, saying they shouldn't do it.

"Well - yes… That would be an idea," Andrew's mum said. She turned to her husband, "Would you like to cut the cake for Andrew?" she asked.

The old man's eyes were fixed on me. A faint smile etched onto his wrinkled, thin face.

"Maybe our guest would like to have the honours? After all, she seems to be pretty keen."

"Okay," I said without hesitation.

"Okay." The old man stood up and reached for a knife, close to the man's still quivering body. He handed it to me, handle stretched out before me. I took a hold of the blade with a shaking hand.

Can you kill them all before they stop you?

#

Christina stood up. All eyes in the room were fixed on her, including the eyes of the so-called 'birthday-cake'. The old man was smiling. He didn't believe she'd go through; none of them did with the exception of Ryan.

He hoped she wouldn't. She moved away from the table and walked towards where the 'cake' had been set up. A couple of dead bodies sat in front of where she needed to be so she pulled them away, letting them slip from their chairs and slump upon the hard floor. Andrew grunted, a smile hidden beneath the painted mask, amused by the corpses sliding from their seats. Christina paid him no notice. She was looking Ryan directly in the eyes. He was shaking his head, mouthing words at her; begging her not to do it. Tears were streaming down his pale face.

"You don't have to do this," he said. "Please." Christina could see he was scared. She could also see the amount of pain he was in; the stitch work at the point of amputation looked angry and sore. A little gore leaking from a tiny point not quite stitched as efficiently as the rest. He was in pain, that's what she kept telling herself. He was in pain but he didn't need to be. It was touch and go as to whether she was going to escape with her life. It was definite that, whether she cut him or not, Ryan wouldn't be. Leaving him there, weeping and scared, was just prolonging his agony. "Please," he continued, "I'm going to be a dad." He said it again to re-emphasise the point, "I'm going to be a dad. Jema - my girlfriend - she is pregnant." Tears continuing to roll down his face as her own eyes welled up.

"Well?" the old man piped up when he realised Christina had frozen on the spot, "Are you going to do it? Andrew would like to eat some of his cake."

Christina looked to the beast at the end of the table. He was rocking from side to side, shaking the whole table with his actions - a beaming smile beneath the rotting face upon his own.

When she spoke, there was a definite shake in her voice, "Did you want to blow your candles out?"

"Of course!" The old lady jumped up from her own chair and took a hold of the lead hanging from her son's bulky neck. She walked towards the cake, the same side as the ever nervous Christina, dragging her son with her. She stopped next to Christina and addressed her son, "Now, do you remember this from last year? You just need to lean forward and give the candles a blow! Make all the little flames go out!" Andrew nodded but didn't move. "Like this," she leaned forward and blew one of the candles, extinguishing the flame in the process. Andrew clapped his hands together, making Christina jump. "Your turn," Andrew's mother pushed her son towards the candles. As he leaned close to Ryan, Ryan screamed out causing him to back away with a frightened grunt from the back of his throat. His mother turned to him and tugged him back towards her with a sharp pull on the lead, "He can't hurt you. You're quite safe… Now come on… Give them a blow."

"Maybe he doesn't want to?" Christina asked; keen to get the whole experience over with.

"Nonsense, he did it last year and enjoyed it." She turned to Ryan, "If you scream again I'll make sure our mutual friend here cuts you in a place you'll find most uncomfortable. Do you understand me?" She turned back to her son, "Come on, blow them out so we can cut the cake. There's a good boy." Andrew leaned in close to Ryan once more. He was just as nervous as Christina and Ryan. He hesitated a moment, unsure as to whether his cake was going to scream out again. A couple of silent seconds passed by and he quickly blew the candles out before retreating back a few steps. His mother clapped once more. "Well done, son!" She turned to Christina, "Now - if you don't mind… You may cut the cake."

Christina looked at Ryan again. Tears still streaming, body still quaking.

"You don't need to do this," he said.

"I'm sorry. I don't have a choice."

"No, she really doesn't!" The mother piped up from a few steps behind Christina.

Christina raised the knife high in the air, both hands on the handle with the blade pointing downwards above Ryan's chest. He was begging her not to do it. He kept telling her over and over that he had a baby on the way; he was going to be a father. Christina closed her eyes tight. Her hands were shaking as a bead of sweat appeared at her forehead. Andrew covered his eyes whilst his mother and father watched on with eager anticipation.

"Do it!" the father hissed.

"Don't!" Ryan begged once more.

Christina opened her eyes and looked down to Ryan again; the man she was going to murder. Tears were starting to well up in her eyes. She kept telling herself that she had to do it. She didn't have a choice. She needed to get the party over with as quickly as possible so they'd let her go. That's what they'd told her. She could go home after the party. She knew the likelihood of that being true was slim but - even so - she had to play along. She cast a hopeful glance to the door. If someone was going to come in and rescue her (them) then now would be a really good time. There was no one there. No sounds from the other rooms, no sounds from outside. Only the heaving breathing of Andrew. She closed her eyes again and brought the knife down hard, straight into Ryan's chest. As the blade pierced his skin, he took a sharp intake of breath. Andrew cheered as Christina pulled the knife out from Ryan's body before plunging it back in again. A little voice in her head telling her to keep doing it until he doesn't move anymore. Keep stabbing him until he is dead. Make it quick. Do that much for him at least. She stabbed him again and again, spray after spray filling the air with a red mist and splashing all around Ryan. The old lady suddenly grabbed Christina's wrists, and held them still for a minute - stopping her from what she was doing. Christina opened her eyes. Ryan was dead. She'd killed him. The old lady shook Christina's wrists from side to side making her drop the bloodied knife onto the table. The tears were streaming down Christina's face uncontrollably. She didn't have a choice. She didn't have a choice. She kept telling herself. She didn't have a choice. It was him or her. Chances are - she knew - it could well end up being both of them.

#

"Sit down," the old lady said to me. I did as I was told, keeping my eyes to the floor; ashamed at myself for what I'd done. I didn't have a choice. It was him or me, I knew that. He was in pain too, psychical pain - not just emotional like me. He was in pain and now he isn't. I took it away from him.

Just as you took away a father from his unborn son.

I can't think of him as being a dad. I can't think of his unborn son. I need to put it from my mind. For my own sanity. I had to do this. I had to. Him or me. I need to move on, don't let it consume me.

You killed someone.

Him or me.

You really think they're going to let you go?

I didn't have a choice.

"I'm impressed," the old man sneered. I didn't need to look up to know he was talking to me. "I think you're going to fit in very well with this family," he continued. I didn't react to what he said. I wanted to. I wanted to say so much but I knew it was pointless. All I would do is anger him - maybe all of them. It's best if I keep my mouth shut and play along. For now at least.

Their son cheered out loud causing me to jump. I turned my eyes from the floor over to where he was still standing next to the man I'd killed.

You did that.

He had a piece of flesh cut from the man's torso in his hand. His mother was standing next to him, cutting off another slither. I gagged when her son bit into the flesh as though it were a piece of cake; a second gag when a piece of fatty liquid ran down the mask's chin.

"Is that nice?" his mother asked. Even she looked disgusted as her son tore another chunk of pink flesh from the clump in his hand. She put a second piece on one of the paper plates dotted around the table and slid it in front of where I sat. I gagged again - more violently this time as I hunched over. Another gag, and another and - I vomited on the floor by my feet. Both the old man and his wife laughed. Their son did nothing, too preoccupied with the tasty treat his loving parents had provided.

Who the fuck are these people?

"Eat it whilst it's warm," the old lady laughed as she continued cutting more from the torso. Andrew dropped the half-eaten piece from his hand and grabbed for Ryan's flaccid cock. His mother slapped his hand with the side of the knife, "We don't eat that bit, dear. We've discussed this before!"

"No son of mine."

I wiped my mouth with the back of my hand and pushed the plate away. I didn't need to see it. I didn't want to see it and I sure as Hell wasn't about to try it, as suggested. Before I'd even finished moving the plate away, a large hand reached out and snatched the meat from it. Andrew. He bit into the flesh - with a rancid squelchy sound - with a feverish hunger. I had to look away. I had to concentrate on something else. The parents thought my reaction to it was amusing but there must have been a time when they were as equally disgusted. How could they allow this?

"Earlier you said some horrible things about your son. If that's how you really feel - how can you do all of this for him?" I asked the still-smirking father. His smile faded from his face within a split second of me finishing the question; angry at me questioning his actions.

"The parties are her idea. Some way of trying to make amends I guess. The only reason he is here though is because I need him to be. I told you - I'm dying. If I want my name to continue then we're going to need to take action. Unfortunately I am too ill to do it myself. My sperm is fried through all the radiation and shit I've had pumped through me. His sperm though...Hopefully it won't be as backward as he is."

I panicked as I realised what he was saying and what it meant for me. They weren't going to kill me. They needed me, just as they needed their son. But it also meant I wouldn't be going anywhere after the party. Not if they're planning what I think they are.

Oh God.

They said I was the guest of honour but I wasn't. I was nothing but another present for their twisted son, just as the man I'd killed had been presented as a birthday cake. I looked over to the door and wondered whether I could make a run for it. Could I get out and find a way out before they catch me? The old couple - the twisted fucks - won't be quick enough for me so long as the doors aren't locked elsewhere but their son… I won't be able to outrun him.

"Which - seeing as the cake is cut - means we might as well continue discussing your role in full. After all, it won't be long now before you have a task to perform," the old man sneered. I felt sick. I couldn't believe I'd been so slow in putting all the pieces together as to why I was here. Without a second thought I jumped up and made a run for the door. No one chased me. I yanked on the handle but the door didn't budge. I tried again. Nothing. Locked? She'd locked it? I didn't realise.

I slowly turned around, back to face the family. They were all staring at me. The old man with that sneer on his face, the mother with a look of bemusement and their son - the freak… I couldn't see under the mask to know the expression. I just hoped it wasn't one of anger.

"Maybe you'd like to take your seat?" the old man stood up and faced me. I walked back over to where I'd been sitting and sat. I can't very well get out without the key which she must still have on her. And I can't try and take it from her, not with all three of them here. I'll never overpower them all. I can't even try. The son's so big… One hit and I'll be out like a light. I felt the uncomfortable-yet-familiar feeling of panic begin to set in once more.

"Well that was very dramatic. Not quite sure what you were hoping to achieve with that but there you go," he laughed.

"Fuck you!" I hissed.

Andrew gasped and raised a bloody hand to his mouth.

"Try and watch the cussing, it upsets the boy." The old man pointed out, "He can be a bit of a handful when he's upset and today's supposed to be his special day." The old man passed behind me as he approached his son,

"You ready to lose your virginity today, boy?! You ready to step up and become a man?!" Andrew grunted with enthusiasm. I'm not sure if it was because he understood what was being implied or whether his enthusiasm was there just because his father was talking to him.

I couldn't help but start to cry, "Why are you doing this to me?" I asked.

"Don't take it so personally. It could have been anyone. Only reason it ended up being you was because of what my wife overheard you talking about in the gas station."

"There was CCTV... They know who you are."

"It was broken and if it wasn't broken then it definitely is now. Come on, we've been doing this same song and dance for a long time now. You really think we wouldn't have checked for cameras?"

Hopes dashed. I am alone.

"We don't have to do this," I pleaded.

"Yes we do. I've already told you I'm on borrowed time. I beat this shit once, but it appears the second time it beat me. Less than a year left, so I'm told."

"Do we have to talk about this?" the old lady asked.

"And I want my name to live on. Clearly that won't be done by me and if I don't step in with fucktard here, it's not going to happen. Hence you're here. You're going to carry his son - or daughter - and my name will live on for a while longer at least. Fingers crossed it won't be a complete fuck-up like Andrew here and it will be normal and go on to have children of their own and so on, so forth...."

"I'm infertile."

"You have a daughter."

"Complications. I can't have anymore."

He smiled, "You're lying." He continued, "Look I wouldn't worry about it - the chances are his sperm is more useless than my own radiated shit… You probably won't even get pregnant but I promise you this - until the day I die - I will keep trying."

"I don't want to," I couldn't stop crying. The thought of what he was saying, the thought of his son on top of me… In me…

Please God just let me die.

"I'm sure if you relax you'll enjoy yourself a little. And don't worry - we'll make sure he is gentle with you so as not to cause any damage. We need you to stick around for a while to give this the best shot possible…"

"You said after the party I could go home."

"After this party you will be home. Just another couple living with the folks. Now - shall we?" the old man reached forward in the flash of an eye and grabbed a handful of my hair, yanking it hard. He pulled me to my feet whilst his wife pushed the plates from our end of the table, leaving the tabletop completely bare with the exception of the creased cloth. Andrew - still with a handful of his cake - watched, wide-eyed and curious.

I screamed.

3.

The old man pushed Christina face down over the bare table. Her feet on the floor, chest pressed against the wooden frame of the tabletop, and her arse pointed in the air. Despite her struggles - and his ailing health - he managed to keep her pinned there with a hand on her back. When it looked as though she were starting to get away from him, he'd pull her head back away from the table and slam it back down again. The old lady watched for a while, before closing her eyes for a moment; flashbacks of her own torment at her husband's cruel hands playing through her mind. Andrew, meanwhile, was excitedly jumping up and down, whooping like the animal he was known to be. The old man hiked the skirt over Christina's rump, revealing the pretty underwear she'd been dressed in. The satin material was the perfect frame to an already impressive rear.

"Oh to be twenty years younger," the old man laughed. He turned to his son, "Here you go, you son of a bitch, Happy Birthday!" He took a step back - keeping a hand pressed down upon the screaming Christina. He expected his son to lunge forward and take what was being offered for him but he didn't move. He just stood there, grunting and rocking. "Well come on then you stupid son of a bitch! Fuck her already!" Christina tried to move away but - once again - had her head slammed down onto the table, stunning her into stillness. "Prime piece of meat here, boy, why aren't you up in there already? Not a fucking queer as well, are you?"

"Please let me go!" Christina screamed, tears streaming. Her head was slammed back down onto the table.

"It's not bad enough that my son needs to be a fucking retard, he has to like the cock as well? Just how fucked up is this brain of yours, boy?" He turned to his wife, "A little help wouldn't go amiss."

The old lady calmly took her son's hand, "Come on Andrew - mummy will show you what to do." She led him up to the table and stood him just behind the dazed girl. "Here - let me help you with this," she said as she started undoing his belt and jeans. With them undone, she pulled them down to round his ankles - exposing his flaccid penis to the cold air.

The old man angered at the sight of the useless tool, "Jesus fucking Christ, you need to sort that out!" he hissed at his wife.

"What do you want me to do?" she asked, shocked that it was down to her.

"What do you think? Get him hard!"

The old lady huffed at her husband before turning her attention to her son. She reached down with her hand and took him in a firm grip. Andrew flinched and looked at his mother, a look of confusion hidden beneath the mask of human flesh. "It's okay," she reassured him. "Close your eyes." He did as his mother told. Christina screamed out again, making Andrew jump once more. "Ssh. It's okay. Ignore the silly girl. Concentrate on what mummy is doing for you." Andrew closed his eyes tight as his father smacked Christina's head back down onto the table with so much force that one of the corpses, resting on a nearby seat, slumped onto the floor. Andrew jumped again. His mother tugged him hard, pulling him close to her once more, before easing her grip and stroking him into an attempted erection. Her husband slammed Christina's head against the table yet again before pulling her underwear down to her ankles, revealing her bare arse and pussy to a confused, grunting

Andrew. One more slam against the desk with Christina's head and the old man quickly positioned his head so that it was level with Christina's dry snatch. Without a second thought he started licking feverishly at it; both for his own sexual gratification and also to ensure it was wet enough to let his son's pathetic cock slide in. The old lady watched as he continued lapping at the girl's cunt. She didn't say anything. She knew better than to question him now, especially when he was in one of these moods. He stood to his full height as Christina started struggling against him. He slammed her head back down again on the table. Blood trickled from a bruised cut on her forehead.

He looked at his wife as he wiped his mouth with the back of his hand, "Tastes better than you ever did and it's not even clean." She bit her lip as she continued stroking their son's penis. The old man looked at it - it wasn't perfectly rigid but he figured that was the best they were going to get. "Bring him here," he ordered her. "Happy Birthday, son!" he said once more as his wife guided her son's penis into Christina's pussy, using her fingers to help open the dazed girl up. Christina yelped in pain as the full girth of both finger and cock entered her. For her troubles, she had her head slammed against the table again.

With the penis deep inside of her, the old lady withdrew her fingers, wiping them on the table cloth. Just because her husband had a taste for fish, it didn't mean she did too. Andrew didn't move. He looked from father to mother and back again, confused as to what was happening.

"Please stop!" Christina begged. She tried to move away, to make Andrew slip out, but the old man reacted in the only way he knew. More blood on the stained table cloth. The old lady saw her son wasn't struggling with what was being asked of him so she moved from his side to behind him. She put a hand on either hip and started moving him backwards and forwards; a fucking motion. His dad smiled when he saw his son was finally hard; his pathetic excuse for a manhood sliding in and out of Christina's cunt. It was clear on the dying man's face that he wished it were him inside her instead of his broken son. With each push forward Christina yelled out which - in turn - caused Andrew to scream out too. The only ones enjoying the scenario being the old man who longed for a son to continue his name, and the old lady who wanted to witness her son's first orgasm inside a woman.

#

Closing my eyes didn't help yet I continued trying. I continued pretending I was somewhere else - at least, I kept trying to. Every time my eyes were closed it just magnified the feeling of him inside of me, making it more intense - pulling me away from where I'd tried to picture myself. Opening my eyes wasn't much better. It made the sensation of him being in me lessen - but not enough to pretend it wasn't happening - but it opened my eyes to what lay before me. A long table, rotting (and rotten) corpses sitting either side - all seemingly looking at me, laughing - and the man I'd killed; holes in his chest and chunks ripped from his body. I knew my crying was making him more apprehensive. I knew it was angering the old couple. Yet I couldn't help it. In my peripheral vision I could make out the shape of the son fucking me, I could make out his mother standing just behind him - guiding him for every motion. I wanted to throw up but somehow managed to keep it within my belly.

Try and close your eyes again.

I closed my eyes and tried picturing myself at a picnic with my daughter and boyfriend. My boyfriend wasn't there. The son. He was there. Naked save for the mask upon his face…

What lies beneath the mask?

…My daughter is with him. I am there too - bent down in front of the monster as he penetrates me from behind. My daughter watches; a look of fascination on her face as she asks him whether he is her dad.

Open your eyes!

The corpses are laughing at me. The old man, laughing. The old woman moving her screaming son faster and faster. Every inch of him is filling me. It stings. Stings like the first time I've been fucked. I screamed out again. He screamed out. The old man roared with laughter. Andrew screamed again, his hands gripped either of my shoulders and pulled me back onto him. A sharp stab from within as I felt his body buckle, starting at his legs. A funny noise escaped his deformed mouth and he started to cry out once more. We all knew what had happened except for him. He had no idea he'd just had an orgasm.

It's inside me.

It was over, thank God it was over, but I couldn't stop crying. I felt his dick slide out of me, no doubt helped by his mother pulling on his hips one last time. Everything sounded distant to me: the laughing, the wailing, the mother telling him to pull his pants up, his dad telling him to quit being such a baby, telling him he was lucky to have had me. I gagged as the scene replayed in my head when I felt a little of him trickle out. I closed my eyes. Easier to take yourself somewhere else when there isn't someone inside of…

My head yanked backwards hard, cracking my neck in the process. The old man still had a clump of my hair in his wrinkled hands. He pulled me to my feet and away from the table. I screamed out but no one cared. He pushed me across the room until I were a few feet from the wall and screamed at me to sit on my bare arse - forcing me down, giving me no option but to do as he said. From the floor, I watched as he reached into his back pocket and withdrew two pairs of handcuffs. The distant sounding voice of his wife asked if he was sure he had the keys still. He told her to fuck off as he clamped a cuff of each around my naked ankles. Too tight. It pinches. I yelped. Without a word - at least none I heard - he pushed me onto my back and, before I knew it, clamped the other side of each cuff to a metal pipe attached to the wall. I was on my back with legs and arse pointed upwards. For a split second I was confused as to why until I realised I was in an uncomfortable, unflattering position which helped the sperm on their way. I cried out, begging him to release me but he either ignored me or my words didn't form as they had in my head and came out as nothing more than another pained scream.

"Half an hour should be long enough," the old lady said from next to the table.

I wailed. I can't stay in this position for half an hour. I can't. The uneven floorboards digging into my already sore back, a painful throbbing from where he'd continually hit me against the table and...

The semen inside of me.

"Please let me go," I begged him. The words definitely formed this time. "Please..."

"Shut up!"

Thoughts rushed through my shattered mind ranging from those of my daughter and boyfriend - in happier times - to the unpleasant realisation that I'd never see them again. The old couple can't release me. They won't release me. They'll keep me here to make sure I am pregnant and then - if I'm not - they'll force me to endure all of this again until I am. And what if there is a point where I never get pregnant? What happens then? Will they keep using me, trying to make it happen or will they kill me?

More tears.

A heavy thumping sound through the floorboards. I turned my head to see Andrew - fully dressed - walking towards me. I flinched as he neared me; worried he was going to try touching me once more considering I had everything on show. He sat next to me and didn't say a word; just the odd sniffle from behind the mask. Did he know what he'd done was wrong? Did he hate this as much as I did? Is he a prisoner too - both in this god forsaken place and in his own mind?

"You two are pathetic," the old man hissed. He walked over to the table and pushed one of the corpses from its chair before taking it for himself. He didn't take his eyes off me. More specifically he didn't take his eyes from my exposed flesh. He was licking his lips. One hand was stroking his leg. I could sense the frustrated desperation that he'd been a part of what had happened. He wished that he'd been in his son's shoes. "Come here," he instructed his wife. She duly went to his side. "There!" he pointed in front of him. "On your knees." She did as she was told. I couldn't take my eyes off of them as he pulled his soft penis out from within his trousers. It was shrivelled, ridiculous looking but it didn't seem to faze him. "Put it in your mouth." The old lady pushed her grey hair out of her face and opened her mouth. The old man stopped her when she inched closer to his still-soft cock. He reached into her mouth,

seemingly gripping either side of her teeth. There was a
clicking noise. He pulled his hand out and with it came
her teeth. I tried not to gag as he set them onto the table
next to where he was sitting. "Now," he let his wife
continue. She put his cock in her mouth and started to
suck it. The old man sighed as he fixed his eyes back
upon me. I didn't move. I didn't dare. I could tell by his
face he wasn't enjoying what his wife was doing, despite
the enthusiastic slurping noises coming from her mouth.
Quick as a flash he shoved her away. "Get the fuck off!"
he yelled at her. She fell back as he stood up to his full
height, revealing his cock had no sign of life in it. He put
it away and stormed across the room to where I was; his
fist clenched into a tight ball. I screamed as he swung,
and closed my eyes ready to receive the blow.

SMACK

Andrew yelled out in pain. I nervously opened my
eyes. The old man was standing next to me raining blow
after blow upon his own son. His son cowered in a ball
despite being able to knock the old man down with ease.

"Get off him!" the old lady screamed as she clambered
back to her feet.

I tried to move, get out of the way, but I was stuck in
position.

Damned restraints.

I closed my eyes and tried to take myself away from it
all.

Go to a happy place.

Silence.

Did it work? Am I in a better place? I nervously
opened my eyes. The old man was standing in front of
me looking at his son with pure hatred in his eyes. His
son was next to me. He too looked up - confused as to
why the hits had stopped coming. I noticed, when he

looked up, that his mask had come away. His face had a number of slashes across it, all stitched with little precision given. His mouth was curled upwards, his teeth twisted… He held his hand up to his dad.

His father spoke in a low pitched voice, "I blame you for everything." His eyes still fixed upon his confused son.

His wife was standing behind him. Slowly he turned to face her. For the first time, I noticed the knife used to cut the cake earlier was sticking from his back.

His wife did that?

"I told you not to hit him!" she said. There seemed to be a hint of remorse in her voice. For why? Because she'd let him hurt them all for so long, for what she'd done to me, or because she'd stabbed her husband? He dropped to his knees before falling face first onto the floor. I could see he was still breathing. Not moving but definitely breathing. She glared at me, "This changes nothing," she said. She made her way over to her son and put a comforting arm around him. "It's okay," she reassured her son who nuzzled in against her body, "It's okay… He won't hurt you anymore."

What about me?

"Please - can you let me down?" I asked, trying my best to appear calm.

The old lady shook her head, "It hasn't been half an hour yet…"

"My back is hurting. Please."

"Shut up! Can't you see we're grieving?!" The old lady moved across to where her husband laid - no longer breathing - and reached into his pocket. She pulled out the rag he'd earlier stashed, along with what was left of the brown bottle. She tipped the contents onto the rag and approached me. "You need to learn when to speak and when not to speak!" she hissed as she held the wet, stinking rag to my mouth. The fumes went to work instantly. I blinked hard, trying to fight it but…

F L A S H E S

The room had no light nor a clock. Day could be night. Night could be day. Christina had no idea as to how she got there. She had no idea what floor they were on. Strong ropes bound her to the bed, naked. Her clothes lay in a pile tossed upon the floor. A chair sat in the corner of the room opposite. Brown bottle and a box of rags on top of that. Uneaten food lay on the floor by one of the chair's leg; maggots crawling over it from where it'd been left to fester. For how long? How many days had passed by? Same routine day in and day out - hard to tell. The old lady comes in with her son. She takes his clothes off for him - sometimes clean underwear, sometimes soiled. She tells him to get on top of Christina and she pushes him inside - sometimes having to stroke him hard first, sometimes sitting back as he finally gets to grips with what needs to be done. Each time Christina cries - her eyes permanently red-raw and soulless, broken - and he cries too; doing what needs to be done to please his hostile mother.

Christina would sometimes scream. The room could be empty but she'd find herself screaming at the top of her lungs; praying that someone, somewhere, would be close enough to hear her cries. He'd scream from within another room. No one would ever come but the mother. A stern look upon her wrinkled face as she'd reach for the brown bottle and another rag. Time for Christina to go to sleep until she were needed once more; not that she was always awake when Andrew penetrated her. She'd wake to his stinking breath assaulting her nostrils, the deformed face - no longer hidden behind rotting flesh -

staring at her own. He'd ejaculate and pull out and Christina would simply lay there - not that she had much choice - with dead eyes fixed to the ceiling. Eyes not unseeing though. Everywhere she looked, he was there. The man she'd killed. Staring back at her with a grin on his face; satisfied she was getting what was deserved of her.

#

Sores covered the back of Christina's body not that anyone saw them, nor cared for them. She knew they were there. She could feel them. Uncomfortable. Dried, stale urine stung the skin on the back of her thighs and her arse from where she'd been forced to wet the bed (and worse). The stench of piss hanging in the air, occasionally making her heave as her brain recalled what it was. Faeces crowning from her sphincter. Repeated pleading to use a bathroom falling upon deaf, uncaring ears. She doesn't need to be clean for what was needed of her. If an answer was presented to her request, it usually ended with, "You give us what we want, you get what you want."

#

Eyes down to the deformed face lapping between her legs. His actions were not of a sexual nature but one of hunger and greed. A taste missed since the birthday party - however long ago that was. Blood around his mouth and a lust in his eyes. A few days of this. Another painful stomach cramp. No baby this month. Maybe next.

#

So much weight lost. Hospital equipment sits by the side of the bed; a bag of fluids hanging from the top. The fluids themselves being slowly drip-fed into Christina's thin arm. A purple and black bruise at the point of entry for the dirty needle, previously used in the arm of an old man. Christina no longer cries nor does she speak nor scream. She simply lies there beaten, broken, damaged, stomach pains suggesting another month is soon to have passed. Sometimes she is dreaming of an escape, other times she is trying to recall the sound of her boyfriend's voice, or her daughter's. All voices of those she once knew lost in the horrors of her life. More often than not, though, she is praying for a death that never seems to come.

#

Eyes down to the old lady. Frail yet dangerous face looking up, expectant. A pregnancy kit in her slightly shaking hand, holding it in the warm stream of urine leaking from Christina's filthy genitals; some splashing on the old lady's skin, not that she cares. She only cares for the result. The beast stands in the corner of the room, trousers round his ankles - semi-erect penis in his gentle, fiddling hand. Laughter from his throat as he takes in what his mum is doing - yet fails to understand the significance. The old lady moves away, the pregnancy kit firmly in her hand and eyes fixed upon it - impatient for the results be they positive or negative.

#

Deformed beast rocking in the corner of the room. Hands raised to ears, drowning out the screaming. Angry

mother repeatedly hitting the restrained Christina -
spiteful words blaming her for the lack of baby.
Christina's eyes closed, her body taking blow after blow;
none of which aimed at her stomach. All at her face;
split lip, bloody nose, blackened eye, bruised cheek.

#

Old lady sits in the corner of the room, tears rolling
down her pale cheek. Broken pregnancy kit amongst the
debris on the floor. Negative, always negative yet the
tears aren't for that. They're for the man she'd once
loved, the man she'd once married and agreed to spend
the rest of her life with. The man she killed. She man she
loathed. The man she'd slowly turned into without
realising. A muttered apology, unheard by Christina
through choice. She'd heard it before and knew that -
tomorrow - the old lady would be back to her wicked
ways once more.

FAST   FORWARD

#

More abuse - verbal and physical.

#

Walking around the corridors, led by a lead around her
neck. Andrew and his mother take it in turn to help her
get some necessary exercise to stop from having her
muscles weaken beyond repair.

#

His penis deep inside her, firing thick jet after thick jet of sticky white semen within her.

#

Praying for death.

#

More fluids - both from the drip and his cock.

#

Praying for death whilst he is deep within.

#

Remembering the daughter. Remembering the lost family. Vowing to see them again as he shoots his load.

#

Another period. Another beating.

#

Muscles so weak now. Arms and legs stick thin. Him still on top. Still pushing in.

#

Old lady screaming.

#

No escape.

#

His breath in her face. Rancid. His cock in her cunt. Rancid.

#

Pregnancy kit.

#

Positive…

CHRISTINA

1.

"You know the drill," the old lady said. She held the pregnancy kit against my vagina and patiently waited. I remember the first time we did this, I couldn't go for ages. She sat there, patiently waiting, but nothing happened. I said it would help if she'd look away. I even told her that I could do it myself if she freed just one of my hands for a minute. She refused though. She said I'd have to go eventually and she was right. I cried the first time as I urinated over her. I felt less than human. Today was different though. Now I didn't care. I didn't care about this, I didn't care when he came inside me, I didn't care about any of it. I just wanted to die; something she was keen to stop me from doing by keeping me going on fluids drip-fed directly into my veins.

Please just let me die.

The urine trickled out of me over the third pregnancy kit she'd made me do. The previous two both coming back as positive. I had no reason to doubt this one wouldn't either. I thought - when she killed her husband - this was all over. I thought she'd finally seen the light and would let me leave on the understanding I wouldn't tell anyone what had happened here. Of course I would have. I would have had the authorities down here so fast. I would have watched from the stands in the courtroom as they got handed down a life sentence, if not the death penalty. I would have laughed as justice was served. I would have told her it would be our secret, though. Just to secure my release. If anything - since her husband died - it got worse.

She sat on the chair in the corner of the room. She was smiling. I knew it was too soon for the results to come back, although it wouldn't be much longer. She was smiling because she was just as sure it would be positive as I was. I wondered what would happen if it was positive. She wouldn't let me go, I knew that much. She'd keep me locked up in this godforsaken room to be sure I wouldn't go and get it aborted. But what then? What after the baby is born? Would I be allowed my freedom? Would I be allowed to go home?

Home? Are they still waiting?

My heart skipped an unwanted beat when my mind drifted to thoughts of home. What about Courtney and Greg? Have they given up waiting for me to come home? Do they presume I am dead like the press presumed the other missing people have been killed? Have they moved on with their lives? Greg has met someone else and married them? I started to cry as I pictured my daughter calling someone else mum.

"Congratulations!" the old lady exclaimed from the corner of the room, perched on her chair. She was waving the stick at me. "You're going to be a mum!" She suddenly burst into tears, "And my boy is going to be a father!" Her son wasn't in the room. I'm not sure where he was. Somewhere outside from where I could hear him crashing around but I couldn't pinpoint the exact location. If he was in the room, I couldn't help but wonder whether he would know what was happening. The old lady's smiled faded from her face. She was looking directly at me and was disturbed by something she'd seen. But what? "Why aren't you happy?" she asked. "You're going to be a mother! That's wonderful news!"

I swallowed hard, "I'm already a mother."

"But now you're going to be a good mother," she said.

"Something you never achieved!" I didn't mean to say it out loud. She threw the pregnancy kit to the floor, jumped up from the chair and slapped me hard in the face.

"I've done my best for that boy. It's not my fault he came out like that."

I laughed, "You're a fine example in the argument between nature versus nurture."

She slapped me again.

"He might have been a little slower than others but do you really think he would have turned out the way he is had you not placed him here? I don't think so."

She slapped me again. The pain spreading through my cheek was nothing compared to the open sores on my back from where I'd not been out of bed. Forced to lie here, rotting for god knows how long.

"I love my son," she spat. She suddenly smiled at me - a smile which sent a cold shiver down my back, "Just as I'm going to love my grandson, or granddaughter."

"And what about the baby?" I asked.

"What about it?"

"You're not getting any younger. You really think you're going to be a fit enough caregiver for the child? I don't. And do you honestly believe your son is going to look after it? He'll probably get confused and try to eat it."

She slapped me again.

"Don't talk about my son like that."

"You know I'm right and the truth hurts."

She went to hit me again but stopped herself when I screamed out, "That's right - keep hitting me, I'm sure the child will turn out perfectly normal." She lowered her hand.

"This is a good occasion. Why are you trying to ruin it," the old lady asked. She returned to the chair and reached for a metal tin hidden beneath it. Whenever she came to the room she had the metal tin with her. Rarely did she open it. I never got a good look inside. The way it rattled, and the fact she'd pull pregnancy kits from it, I just presumed it was filled with more of the kits. She set the tin on the chair and opened it. Can't see inside.

"What are you doing?" I asked.

She pulled a sharp knife from the box and turned to me, "Can't very well keep you lying there for the next nine months," she said. "We need you fit and healthy for this baby." Her tone had completely changed. The woman with multiple personalities. She walked over to me and put the knife against the rope holding me to the bed. "Andrew!" she called out. Loud, heavy footsteps bounded their way down the corridor and the door swung open. Her son was standing there, looming in the doorway. He started to fiddle with his trousers, no doubt expecting to do what has been asked of him on a near daily basis. "No, no, you silly boy. I need you to stand there and watch her. She's pregnant! You're going to be a dad!" He started rocking from side to side, grunting excitedly. I don't believe he understood her; an excited reaction to the tone in her voice. "We can't very well leave her here. We need to start building her strength up for the coming months!" she started hacking at the ropes.

This is it.

"Don't try anything," she told me. The tone in her voice had changed once again. The harsh old lady was back. The excited, happy one gone. "You don't want to force my hand." The knife cut the first rope. I dropped my arm to my side. It feels so heavy, so useless. She started on the second rope. "You might have been stronger before, when you were eating properly - but

216

your body is weak now. Remember that. But don't worry - I will help you build your strength and I will help you give birth to my grandson…So long as you don't try anything stupid." My body was weak. She only let me off the bed every other day to work my muscles… Of course my body was weak.

"I won't."

My second arm was freed and - just as I had with the other - I lowered it to my side. The old lady put the knife down on the floor and helped pull me up the bed so that I was in a sitting position; my back to the wall. My whole body ached, every joint screamed. She reached under the bed and pulled a thin, grimy looking sheet out which she then placed over my naked, bruised body.

"You shall not be permitted out of this room unless accompanied," she said. "Either myself or Andrew will always be close-by and the door shall remained lock. I will let you use a shower and a bathroom whenever you wish but - again - it shall be under supervision. Food - we can get rid of the drip so long as you start eating. I shall cook you healthy meals. If there is something you would like, you may request it on the weekends - otherwise you will be eating what we eat. Do you understand?"

I nodded.

"And?" she raised an eyebrow.

"Thank you?" I said, confused as to what she was waiting for.

"You're very welcome. And welcome to the family."

"When can I see my family?" I asked despite already knowing what the answer was most likely to be.

"We are your family now."

"I have a daughter."

"You had a daughter. We've spoken about this."

I didn't push her further. There was no sense in angering her.

"Now," she continued, "do you want a sandwich? I'm about to make tuna and cucumber for Andrew and I if you would like one too."

"Yes please," I said. I had no intention of eating it. I just needed some alone time to think things through.

The old lady nodded and collected the assortment of items she'd brought with her into the room, including the knife, unfortunately. She walked to the exit and stopped by her son, "Are you staying with her or coming with mummy?" she asked. He pointed to me. "Suit yourself. Don't let her out of the room." The old lady walked past her son, leaving the two of us alone. He didn't say anything (of course he didn't). He just stood there, looking at me. I shifted uneasily, wondering as to whether I could get by him and - if I could - how easy it would be to find the exit.

He grunted and pointed at me.

Keep him calm. Keep him happy.

"Hello," I said. The more I spent time with him - even after what he'd been doing to me - the more I realised he wasn't the monster here. He wasn't to blame for any of this. He was simply a product of his upbringing. The real monster was his mother. His father too, when he was alive. "How are you today?" I asked him, trying to keep calm.

He grunted.

"Did you understand what your mum said about being a dad?" I didn't know whether he understood the words I was saying. Part of me didn't think he did. But I was sure he understood the tones people used. If they spoke nicely to him, he reacted well. If they got upset, so did he. I purposefully kept my voice friendly. "We're going to be a family," I continued. "You and me, with a little baby. A baby!"

He grunted again and rocked from side to side before moving over to the chair. He took a seat and pointed at me again. I wasn't sure what he wanted so I continued talking.

"I hope it's a boy this time. I've got a girl at home. It would be nice if she could have a brother to play with, don't you think?"

He grunted.

Carefully - and slowly - I stood up. My legs were shaky. I had to keep hold of the bed to stop myself from crumbling to the floor. My muscles are so weak. He stood up too, suddenly alert.

"It's okay," I reassured him, "I'm not going anywhere. I'm just standing up. Fed up of lying down on the bed," I smiled at him. He smiled back but didn't stand down.

That's okay. You're not going anywhere yet.

Even if he did stand down - the muscles in my legs are so weak, I wouldn't get far. I need to be sensible. I need to bide my time.

"Here we go," the old lady spoke from the corridor. She walked into the room with a tray of food; three plates of sandwiches. One for each of us. She set the tray down and handed me a plate. "Nice to see you up and about," she said. "How are the legs?"

"Sore."

"To be expected." She handed a plate to Andrew. He snatched it and started eating the sandwich from it, holding the plate close to his mouth. She sat on the edge of the bed and started eating her own sandwich. I looked at mine with suspicion.

You're pregnant. It won't be poisoned.

I remembered her son so readily eating human flesh. I sniffed the sandwich. It smelt like tuna?

219

"What's wrong?" the old lady noticed my sniffing of the sandwich. "You don't trust me?"

"Can you blame me."

"I can assure you there's nothing wrong with the sandwich," she said.

I changed the subject, "What if the pregnancy falls through? Sometimes - especially when someone has been through a stressful time - people can have miscarriages early on."

"Then we will try again," she said. She took another bite of her sandwich. I didn't ask if that meant I needed to be restrained again. I didn't need to know. I won't be here much longer. I won't. I'm not sure how I'll get out yet but - first opportunity - I'll make a run. And so what if he catches up with me and kills me? I'm not sure what will happen when I give birth. I'm not sure if they will want me around still or whether they'll just kill me, happy they have the baby. I don't care. I don't want to carry their child. I want it out of me. I want it dead - and if that's my abortion then I need to get out of here sooner rather than later.

"Nothing to say?" she asked.

I played the part necessary, "Well hopefully it won't come to that," I told her.

She smiled.

2.

The door creaked open to reveal the old lady standing there. She had a towel in her hands. I'm not sure how long I'd been left on my own for after sharing lunch with them but - at a guess - I'd say it was about thirty minutes. Maybe less.

"I thought you might want a shower," she said.

"I would." Not a lie. I stank. Sweat, faeces, urine. You name it, I'm caked in it.

"Remember…"

I stopped her in her tracks, "I won't try anything."

"Well that's good." She smiled and handed out the towel. I took it. "Are you okay to walk or would you like me to fetch the wheelchair?"

My legs hurt. They felt weak. I needed to get them moving again. I needed to use the muscles once more. It won't be long before I am trying to get away. If I get out of the building - I could have miles to go before I find civilisation. The mere thought of running miles, now, made me feel sick. I knew it would be a struggle.

Would you rather stay?

"I'll try and walk, thank you."

She'd taken the I.V drip from my arm after our sandwich earlier. It had felt so good to get the foreign body from my vein that I could have hugged her. I nearly did for a moment too - temporarily losing my senses. With the towel in hand I walked from the room and into the corridor. We were still upstairs it seems.

That's good. You won't need to find your way out of the maze downstairs.

"Which way is it?" I asked her. She pointed me down the corridor to a room at the far end.

"That way."

I started walking. She was walking close behind me - her arms outstretched towards me. I wasn't sure whether she was going to try and grab me if I ran or whether she was holding her arms up to catch me if I fell.

"Where's Andrew?" I asked.

"Oh, he's around." I knew she was reluctant to give me an answer. Again, she was protecting herself. Together we walked through to the end of the corridor and entered the shower room. I'm not sure what the large building was used for before but the long room had a line of showers along the wall. There were no windows in the room. "Take your pick," she said. She stood by the door and watched as I look along the shower heads, each one separated by a brick wall partition for a little privacy. "Oh, you might need this," she reached into her pocket and pulled out a small bar of soap. I thanked her as I took it to one of the partitions in the middle of the room; the best one for privacy, I thought. I hung my towel on a hook which stuck out from the end of the partition wall and stepped up to the shower. From where I was, I couldn't see the old lady. I knew she was there though. I knew she wouldn't leave me alone.

It doesn't matter. You can over-power her. This is your best opportunity.

It would be better if I knew where her son was but the little voice in my head was right; this was the best chance I had of getting away. I put my hand on the faucet but made no effort to twist it round in order to get the water flowing from the shower head.

"Can you help me?" I asked.

"What is it?"

"I can't turn the water on. It's stuck."

"Try another one."

Shit.

I stepped into the next shower and tried the same trick. "This one won't turn either."

"I used that one earlier, I know it's fine." The old lady sounded annoyed.

"Well could you help me then please? You've done it up really tightly."

"I'll get my son."

"There's no need to disturb him yet," I said, trying to act cool. "You did it up - chances are you can undo it."

The old lady walked over to me. I put some effort in to make it look as though I was trying to turn the water on.

"Get out of the way then," she snapped.

I stepped back from the shower and let her in. I reached for the towel hanging on the peg. I put opposite ends of the towel in either hand and with adrenaline surging through my body - and her back to me - I hooked it over her head and yanked back against her scrawny throat. I held her - squirming - against my body. She pushed back and I stumbled, slamming my back against the opposite wall. I didn't let go of the towel though. I kept it pulled back - hard - against her neck as she continued to gasp for air; her arms flailing around all over the place. I tugged harder as she reached under the towel, squeezing her fingers between cloth and skin. This needs to happen quicker. If she raises the alarm, he'll come. I swung my body around, swinging her round in the process, and slammed her against the wall. I swung back the other way and slammed her into one of the partition walls. I let go of the towel and she crashed to the floor. I fell on top of her and grabbed her head, slamming it down onto the hard tiled floor - not just once but again and again and again. Dirty white tiled floor. Cracks appeared. Blood splattered. I kept slamming her head down - just as her husband had done to me once upon a time - even after she'd stopped fighting me.

Murderer.

I had to kill her. I didn't have a choice.

Always an excuse.

I had to.

Just like you had to kill the man at the birthday party?

They made me do it.

Always someone else to blame.

Fuck you! I can't stay here any longer. I can't. I don't want this baby inside of me. I lifted the old lady's head one last time and slammed it back down onto one the tiles. Her eyes were open and her forehead was cut wide open showing a hint of skull underneath the ripped flesh. She won't be getting back up. I stood up and turned for the door. I froze.

"M O M M A ? ! "

#

Christina was standing by the old lady's body. Her eyes wide with fear. Andrew was standing in the doorway, blocking her exit.

"Momma?" he repeated.

"She's asleep," Christina said, trying her best to keep her voice calm and soothing. In her head she was hoping what she thought earlier was right; he understands little in the way of words and instead behaves according to tone heard. If she is calm, he is calm. Andrew lurched towards her - she backed up against the wall. He stopped at the body of his dead mum. He reached down and picked her up, standing her up. He let go and she slumped to the floor, cracking her head once more.

"Momma?"

He picked her up and tried again. And - again - she slumped to the floor.

"Momma?"

"She's really tired," Christina said. "She'll wake up soon enough. It's okay."

Andrew dropped to his knees by his mother's body. Silence filled the room for a moment until he suddenly screamed out loud. He reached down and pulled his mother's body close to him, holding her tight. Christina didn't move. She didn't care. She knew he understood his mother wasn't sleeping. The reaction proved as much. He knew she was dead and - when he looked up at Christina - he knew she was responsible.

"I had to," Christina said. "She wanted to kill the baby." She patted her stomach, "Baby? She wanted it dead."

"NO!" Andrew yelled.

"I was protecting our baby!"

"NO!"

He stood up to his full height and screamed again, causing Christina to flinch. She couldn't go further back. One way into the room and one way out, and that was past Andrew.

"Momma!" he screamed again.

#

He's going to kill me. This is it. I'm dead. I can't just stand here and wait for him to come to me. I need to try to get away at least. He isn't a bad person. He hasn't hurt anyone that I have seen anyway. It's always been them. It's always been his mum and dad. They're the bad people. He is as much a victim as I am. Maybe he'll let me go? Maybe he won't care that I get away?

Are you sure?

I don't know but I have to try. I can't stand here waiting for him to come to me. I can't. I took a deep breath. It's now or never. I have to do this. I have to try.

#

Christina seized her opportunity. She ran at Andrew in the hope of ducking past him at the last possible second. He swung his arm and slammed it against her throat dropping her to the floor like a sack of spuds. He reached down and scooped her up in his arms, holding her a foot off the floor and close to his body - one arm around her waist and one arm around her neck.

"Don't leave!" he screamed again and again. "Don't leave! Don't leave!" Tears of anguish, pain, and even fear spilled from his eyes; scared at the prospect of being left alone. "We family!" Christina was clawing at his arms, kicking aimlessly with her feet. Her face was turning blue as she struggled to breathe the required oxygen in. Andrew didn't understand, he simply held her tighter, stopping her from getting away and leaving him to an unfamiliar solitude. "Don't leave! Don't leave!" He dropped to his knees, holding her still close to him. "Don't leave!" He gave her another tight squeeze as though to reiterate his need to keep her close. Something snapped. Christina stopped fighting. Her body went limp. Her head flopped as far forward as the arm around her broken neck permitted. Andrew didn't let her go. He sat there, crying, holding her corpse. "Don't leave. Please. No leave me alone."

Christina had already left.

The room was still. The room was silent. Bar the soft whimpering of a misunderstood giant.

226

E P I L O G U E

ONE YEAR LATER

A YOUNG BOY

NAMED SEAN

Sean fell through the thick bush laughing hysterically. Pushed by his friend - John - he hadn't expected to fall through. He thought he'd simply bounce off of the shrubbery - hence he didn't try protecting himself. He landed on the unkempt grass of a large meadow with a heavy thud; a landing which winded him. John crawled through the bush, after his friend. He too was laughing. He dropped a football from under his arm and helped his friend up to his feet.

"Are you okay?" he asked. "I'm sorry, I didn't think you'd fall right the way through."

"You're a dick!" Sean laughed as he brushed himself down.

The boys were in their teenage years. Aged sixteen. Both of them were dressed in uniform; that of the school they were playing truant from.

"Whoa! Look at that!" Sean said as he looked up, looking over his friend's shoulder.

"Yeah fuck off am I falling for that." He expected to turn around and get shoved back. If the shoe were on the other foot - it would have been a trick he tried for himself. Get his friend distracted and then push him as hard as he could in order to send him crashing to the floor. He wasn't born yesterday.

"Look!" Sean pointed. "I'm not joking."

"I'm not falling for it!"

Sean grabbed his friend by the shoulders and spun him around on the spot. Behind him - a little further down the messy meadow - was what looked to be an abandoned warehouse of sorts. Sean didn't wait for his friend's reaction as he started running towards it.

"Wait up!" John called after him, as he too started to run towards the seemingly derelict building, leaving the football where he'd dropped it when he helped Sean up to his feet.

"I know this place," Sean said as he neared. He stopped running and froze on the spot, staring at the warehouse. "I know it. It was in the news last year."

"What are you talking about?"

"You don't remember?"

"Remember what?"

"The disappearances in the papers and on the television. All those people. I think this is the building where they found all of the dead bodies. I think."

"Shut up."

"I'm telling you the truth, asshole." He playfully punched his friend on the arm.

"You're bullshitting."

"Nope. I can't remember how many dead people they found inside but there was a lot. I remember that much."

"Well what else did it say?"

"I can't remember."

"You are such a fucking bullshitter."

"I'm not. Come on. Let's try and find a way in."

The windows were boarded up. There were notices dotted around the brickwork warning that trespassers would be prosecuted if found and - not only that - also stating the building was condemned; unsafe for entry.

"I'm not going in there," John stayed put as Sean approached the building. "It looks like it's liable to fall down at any minute."

"Come on. Don't be a pussy."

"I'm not going. I'm not going to be one of those assholes who goes into a building only to get butchered. Don't you pay attention in horror films? I've seen too many to know what happens next in this situation."

"It's okay, they think the people responsible for all the murders were actually among the corpses they found."

"What? How would they even fucking know that?"

"Science and shit, I guess? Come on, there's nothing to be worried about. Even if the people who did it weren't among the dead - they're long gone. This place was on the news for like a fucking month."

"You're a dick. I'm not going in there. Let's just get the ball and go already. Place gives me the fucking creeps."

"Come on, it'll be a laugh."

"No. What if something happens? One of us will have to go and get help and then our parents will know we weren't in class. Let's go."

"No. Not until you admit you're a chicken."

"What?"

"I'm not going until you admit you're too scared to come inside with me."

"I'm not too scared."

"Great! Let's go in!"

"No."

"Admit it."

"Fuck you."

"Either admit it or we go in. It's up to you."

"Fine. Okay. Whatever."

"Say it."

"I'm too scared to go in there. Fine. Happy?"

Sean started to laugh, "You're such a pussy."

"Fuck you. Come on, let's get the ball."

"Where is it?"

They turned around just in time to see the football roll towards them. There, standing in the distance, was the shape of an overly tall man.

Sean asked, "Who's that freak?"

MONSTER

T H E   E N D

MONSTER

Manufactured by Amazon.ca
Acheson, AB

11472287R00131